After all the his voice.

"Yes, Pierce. How can I help you?" She allowed a tinge of frost in her tone.

He sighed. "Look, Silvia, I know I hurt you, but I need help and you're the only one I really know. Plus, Kianna likes you."

"What kind of help?" She wasn't touching his admission of having hurt her.

"You were right. My mom's health isn't great." He paused and cleared his throat. "I know you're busy with the restaurant, but I can't saddle Mom with Kianna's care. Would you be able to help out?"

"Help out how?"

"Maybe you could help take her to school and pick her up on the days when I have to work with the cattle."

He sounded like he was holding his breath waiting for her answer.

She didn't want to be around Pierce. But the fact was they lived in a small rural area and she couldn't escape meeting up with him. Plus, the sadness on that little girl's face tugged at her heart.

She sighed. "I'll see what I can do."

Nancy J. Farrier is a bestselling, award-winning author of over thirty-five books. Nancy has written both historical and contemporary fiction, as well as nonfiction for the Christian market. Her Southwest fiction is filled with characters who face real-life issues, which she hopes will encourage her readers. Nancy lives in Arizona in the Sonoran Desert and loves the sunshine and most of the time enjoys the heat. She lives with her husband, cats and dog. Nancy enjoys early morning hikes, spending time with her family, reading and going to church.

Books by Nancy J. Farrier

The Veteran Rancher's Return

Visit the Author Profile page at LoveInspired.com.

THE VETERAN RANCHER'S RETURN

NANCY J. FARRIER

LOVE INSPIRED
INSPIRATIONAL ROMANCE

LOVE INSPIRED®

INSPIRATIONAL ROMANCE

ISBN-13: 978-1-335-62142-9

The Veteran Rancher's Return

Recycling programs
for this product may
not exist in your area.

Love Inspired
22 Adelaide St. West, 41st Floor
Toronto, Ontario M5H 4E3, Canada
www.LoveInspired.com

HarperCollins Publishers
Macken House, 39/40 Mayor Street Upper,
Dublin 1, D01 C9W8, Ireland
www.HarperCollins.com

Printed in Lithuania

But ye are a chosen generation, a royal priesthood, an holy nation, a peculiar people; that ye should shew forth the praises of him who hath called you out of darkness into his marvellous light.
—*1 Peter* 2:9

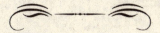

For all those who have suffered hurt, wounded by another. May this story help to heal some of that hurt by allowing love to heal the wounds.

Chapter One

Miles of grassland stretched on both sides of the road, and in the distance Arizona's White Mountains wove in pine-covered slopes, their call a visceral tug on Pierce Forester's heart. His home. The place where he'd grown up. The place he'd never wanted to leave. The place where he'd fallen in love.

The home he'd turned his back on in a fruitless effort to save that love.

Fourteen years since he'd returned, except for brief visits when he'd had leave from the military. Even then, he rarely stayed for very long. For his siblings' graduations. When his father had his first heart attack and surgery.

But not when his father died last spring. He'd missed the funeral. Missed being the support his mother needed. The strong older brother to his three siblings. The one his dad used to count on to be there.

Instead, he'd been recovering in a hospital in Germany from a mission gone wrong. His family didn't know that. They thought he'd abandoned them once again. They'd thought that about him for fourteen years. But now, he was back and ready to step into his father's shoes.

Whether or not those shoes fit.

He was here to give up his wandering and step into the life he'd wanted and trained for from the start—running the family ranch. He hoped his family would welcome him back, but that wasn't a given. They'd been hurt and angry when he left home in a futile attempt to prove himself. That hadn't worked out, not the way he'd intended. Silvia, the love of his life, had moved on, not giving him another thought—what else could he think? After all, she'd changed her phone number and hadn't returned his emails. Maybe he should have tried social media. But that wasn't him.

"Unca Purse, I'm thirsty. I want juice."

He ripped his gaze from the mountains to glance in the rearview. Kianna. His soon-to-be-adopted daughter, a five-year-old who'd regressed since her parents' deaths. His to raise because he'd been named guardian. He swallowed a few times as his throat tightened. "Almost to town, sweetie. We can stop for a snack and a bathroom. I'll refill your water then. You can have juice when we get to Grandma's. Okay?"

Please, please, let that be okay. He'd learned the hard lesson about giving her juice in the car. What a sticky mess. He'd been thankful for a mother with two small children when she pointed out how to replace the ruined car-seat liner so Kianna would be comfortable again. Washing it wasn't an option when they were on the road driving cross-country.

"Cows." Kianna's excited yell jarred him from his thoughts. He glanced at the pasture on her side to see a herd of horses grazing in the distance. He chuckled. Not only was the prodigal returning to the ranch, but he was also bringing a child who didn't immediately know the difference between a horse and a cow. Granted, they were mostly dots on a hillside. Still, his family would love this.

Or at least, the family he remembered from his childhood would. Being in the Special Forces meant he'd spent a lot of time incommunicado, which had only exacerbated the tension between him and his siblings. They'd never agreed with his decision to leave the ranch, after all. He knew the twins, Ashlyn and Quinn, lived in LA now, and his mom had been vague about his brother Caleb.

At least his mom was waiting for him and Kianna, anxious to meet her new granddaughter.

Houses flashed past. Ashville, Arizona, his home town. Some defunct businesses and a few new ones he hadn't seen before. Coltrane Restoration. Mountain Memories—an antique store. He flipped on his blinker to turn into the Chuckwagon parking lot and noted a new bakery across the street called Sweet & Savory. A few people waited in line, so it must be doing okay. Many businesses in small towns were teetering on the edge of going under.

He prayed the ranch wasn't one of them. But there had been something in his mom's voice yesterday.

"Unca Purse, are we here?"

He shut off the engine and turned to smile at her. For the first time in the weeks since she'd being orphaned, her eyes showed a little interest in her surroundings. His heart warmed.

"We are here, sweetie. Let me come get you." He hopped out and opened the back passenger door. Her lips tilted in what was almost a smile. It didn't reach her eyes. They still held a sadness he didn't know how to combat. His enemies had always been physical beings, not something emotional. How was he supposed to slay dragons for this little girl if those dragons were mist and smoke?

The few steps it took to enter the restaurant brought him back fourteen years. He glanced along the wall to the booth in the rear. A young couple sat there laughing and sharing a plate of fries. He rocked back on his heels. Fourteen years ago, that would have been him and Silvia. His chest tightened, and he struggled to draw in a breath.

Silvia. The thought of her still hurt. At least she didn't live here anymore.

"Pierce Forester, is that you?" Jeanne Wilson, longtime cook for Chuckwagon, peered out from the kitchen. "I do believe it is." She slipped through the double doors and came to give him a hug.

"Jeanne. How are you?" He squeezed Kianna's hand as her fingers tightened on his. Fear dogged this little girl everywhere now, no matter how much he reassured her he wasn't going anywhere. He'd be here for her.

"We're doing the best we can. You heard about Pete, didn't you?" Jeanne's long silver hair, caught back in a large barrette at the base of her neck, released a curl to dance at the side of her face. Her eyes held a similar sadness to Kianna's.

"Pete? No. Is everything okay?" Pierce caught her hand with his free one. The familiar scents of coffee and grease hung in the air, while dread pounded in his gut. Pete. Who owned Chuckwagon. Silvia's father.

"He had a stroke." Jeanne tightened her grip on his hand before he said anything. "He'll be okay. He's…"

"Unca Purse." The small voice beside him held a note of panic as his charge danced in place.

He glanced down at the desperation evident in the thin line of Kianna's mouth.

"Ah, you go ahead. I'll whip up your favorite burger and something for the girl." Jeanne's forehead crinkled as she looked at Kianna. Then she nodded toward the restrooms and pushed back into the kitchen.

By the time he and Kianna returned to the counter, Jeanne was bringing out a burger for him, a grilled cheese for Kianna and a mound of fries for them to share. Kianna's eyes rounded at the sight of the food. He hadn't meant to get lunch here, but the smell reminded him he hadn't eaten since before daybreak.

He slid into a booth with Kianna next to him. Jeanne placed the plates in front of them. "What about drinks? Soda? Milkshake?"

"Maybe just water. The last time I got Kianna a milkshake it gave her a tummy ache."

"Ah, maybe some lactose intolerance. You have to watch for those things." Jeanne hurried off, then brought back water for them and a cup of coffee for herself. She sat down across from them just as Pierce finished praying for the food. He waited until Kianna picked up half her grilled cheese sandwich and took a bite. Then he picked up his burger and faced Jeanne.

"What happened with Pete? Where is he?"

"He spent a couple of days in the hospital in Show Low. He's home now and has a nurse coming by to help him with a few things. Also, a therapist stops by."

"How bad was the stroke?" Pierce had trouble thinking of the vibrant, hard-working Pete Durham being incapacitated with anything.

"He's having a little trouble talking. Small motor skills are hard for him. I was out there yesterday and he's made great progress. He's hoping to be back at the restaurant in a couple of weeks. His health care workers are a little less optimistic."

"Well, it's nice he has you here. You know this restaurant about as well as he does." Pierce put a few fries on Kianna's plate and squirted a puddle of ketchup near them.

"Oh, it's not just me." Jeanne drained her coffee and stood as a family of four came through the door. "Silvia came back to help."

Dust billowed up behind her SUV as Silvia Rowland headed for the next stop for her lunch deliveries. She liked this part of the business her dad had started. He hadn't offered lunches to the surrounding ranches when she was younger, and driving through the Northern Arizona countryside relaxed her like nothing else. Her memories here were free of the devastating loss she'd endured recently, because her husband and son had never visited her home or met her parents. Her heart twisted. Why had she never brought Keith and Steven here? After the accident that claimed their lives, she'd regretted that choice.

Her mother had been gone for five years, and Silvia swallowed the pill of regret most days. Her mom and dad never met their son-in-law or grandson. Never got to know Steven's bright smile and zest for life that reflected his father so much. How had she let that happen?

She shook off the depressing thoughts and slowed to turn into the ranch driveway, a long dirt track that led back to the house, barns and cabins for the crew. Dust billowed up around her car as she slowed, but she still noted the overhead sign with the stylized FR, standing for Forester Ranch. Her heart blipped every time she saw that symbol. Every time she remembered her high school days.

Every time she remembered Pierce Forester.

But she would not think about him. Not anymore. They'd both gone their separate ways. They both led productive lives but hadn't kept in touch other than through the grapevine— her father and his mother. So why did being back here feel like immersing herself in thoughts of Pierce just as she had in high school?

They'd been inseparable. Studying together. Eating together at Chuckwagon under her parents' watchful eyes. Attending church. Going to school games—although at most of those she sat on the bleachers and cheered for Pierce, the best athlete the school had seen in years.

The SUV hit a bump, and she forced her attention back to the road. This had been a wet year, and while the county maintained the dirt roads and did a decent job, most of the ranchers were busy with winter preparation and hadn't gotten around to dragging the lanes leading to their houses. The rains had wreaked their havoc. The Forester lane was worse than most, probably because Brenda Forester was on her own with none of her children close. The job of running their ranch fell on her frail shoulders, and from what Silvia knew from her visits with Brenda, things weren't going well.

Brenda knew what she was doing. She'd run the ranch with her husband for many years. Of course, her health hadn't been so fragile then. She'd had a trustworthy foreman who'd since passed away. The next foreman had been given much-needed walking papers, and one of the ranch hands took the job. Grady had a good heart but not enough experience or training.

By the time she reached the barn, the trail of dust had subsided. At least the cowhands kept this part of the lane watered, so there wasn't as much dirt to deal with in the house and cabins. She climbed from her car and stretched as she looked around. This had to be the most beautiful ranch in Arizona. The hills dipped and swelled as they led up to mountain slopes covered in juniper on the lower areas and tall pines and spruce as they gained altitude. The white bark of aspen trees in the upper slopes added to the beauty.

And the scent. She'd been all over the world for her work and nothing smelled quite as good as home. The pine. The fresh air. The grass. It all combined to make her wonder why she left in the first place. Would she even be back here if it wasn't for the accident that cost the lives of her family, combined with her father's failing health?

That didn't matter. She was here to help her father until he was back on his feet and able to run his business. That was it. Once he was back to normal, she'd head out of the country to finish the trips she and Keith had lined up so she could complete their book on adventure traveling.

Who was she kidding? She'd come here to recover from losing her family. Not to mention she'd been avoiding her agent and editor, the ones in charge of seeing that she finished the book she and Keith had started. But she'd lost the joy she once found in their adventures and writing about them.

Leaving had been her plan for as long as she could remember. She'd traveled the world, experiencing adventure after adventure, fulfilling all her childhood longings. She had no regrets. Well, except for not bringing Steven back so her parents could meet their grandson. But she did not regret following her dream. She. Regretted. Nothing.

Liar. What about Pierce?

Moot point. Because Pierce was the man who refused to leave this ranch for her. The man who broke her heart when he put her second. The man who ended up leaving, anyway, traveling the world with his fellow soldiers. That man needed to stay gone. Because she didn't want to see him again. Ever.

"Hey, Miss Silvia. You need some help?" Grady sauntered toward her.

She shut her door and hit the button to open the hatch. "I've got this, Grady, but thank you." She lifted out the wagon she used to transport the lunch boxes and set what she needed in the bed. Drinks, lunch boxes, new menus for next week. They all fit in the wagon, which was easy to pull over rough terrain. One of her dad's best investments.

"Here, I'll take that for you." Grady took the handle from her. He grinned, his pale face stubbled with blond, offset by twinkling eyes that were the washed-out blue of an early morning sky.

"Thanks." Silvia walked alongside the wagon, making sure

the load balanced and nothing fell. These men were always asking for dates. They were nice enough, but she didn't date. She had no interest in dating. Her heart had been shattered by that cliffside in Switzerland.

Grady led the way into the largest cabin, which had been set aside as a cookhouse and dining area. Fifteen men lounged around the tables, chatting and laughing. More would head in for their lunches soon.

Many ranches were struggling to stay afloat, and hiring a full-time cook had proved expensive. Her father and a couple of the ranchers discussed ways to help, leading Pete to start the box-lunch program. The ranchers ordered lunches from Chuckwagon and paid for delivery service or sent someone to pick them up. That way, the cowboys had a nutritious meal and then they would take turns fixing the evening meal for everyone. The practice cut costs for the ranchers and helped her dad.

And since his stroke, her dad had needed someone to take over his route for delivery. Silvia much preferred the alone time of driving and delivery to the constant hubbub of the restaurant. Out here there was a modicum of peace that she hadn't found anywhere else. And these days, she'd do almost anything for a little peace.

As she stepped through the door, there was a chorus of greeting—"Silvia" and "Hey, Ms. Silvia"—as all the men dropped their conversations and turned her way. Disconcerting, but she was getting used to it.

"Lunch is here." Silvia lifted the container of boxes out and carried it to an empty table while Grady set out the drinks. The cowboys gathered around to grab their meals and each of them gave her a quick pat on the shoulder, a nod and thanks, or a hug. The hugs almost felt natural now, but she still kept a bit of distance from each hugger type.

"What do we have today?" Grady opened his box. "Roast beef?"

"It's whatever you checked on the menu." Silvia pushed out a smile and shook her head. "You ask that every time. Maybe you should make a note on your phone about what you've ordered for each day."

The men laughed. Some lowered their heads to say a quick prayer before they dug in.

Silvia held up the menu sheets for the next week. "Don't forget to pick up one of these and fill it out. I'll get them tomorrow. And put your name at the top so we know who is who—Grady." She sent the cowboy a mock glare. The room erupted in laughter.

She took the box that had held the lunches and set it back in the wagon, along with the leftover drinks. She always brought more than enough and a variety, since this wasn't a choice on the menu.

She grabbed the handle of the wagon and lifted her hand to wave at the room, when the silence registered. All the men were staring at the door instead of eating.

Silvia turned. Her breath caught. Her heart thudded. She must be seeing things. Her earlier thoughts had come to life. Except he was older, more muscular and ruggedly handsome, instead of the good-looking boy she'd fallen in love with.

Pierce Forester. In the flesh.

Chapter Two

"Pierce." His name slipped out. She had no power to snag it back or swallow the myriad of emotions carried in his name. Longing. Regret. Love.

No. No. No. Anger should be right at the top of the list. She did not love Pierce Forester. Not anymore. Maybe she never had. He certainly hadn't loved her or he wouldn't have let her leave by herself. His vow to her meant next to nothing then and even less now.

Her fingers tingled, numb from her tight grip on the wagon handle. She gave a tug, planning to sweep past Pierce without giving him a second glance. But then, her gaze caught movement and she looked down.

A young girl clung to Pierce's leg, her hair pulled into a ponytail that was off-kilter. Tiny curls had escaped and framed her round face. Wide, caramel-colored eyes stared at Silvia and then all the men in the room.

Pierce had a child. Her throat closed so tight she might never breathe again. A stab of pain hit her heart. Steven. This girl was about the same age Steven had been. How was this fair, that Pierce had a beautiful child while hers had been ripped from her life?

She had to get out of here. Shove her way past the mountain that was Pierce and escape. If she stayed here, she'd end up a puddle on the floor. Just a worthless mess of emotion that they'd have to scrape up and toss on the manure heap. Then where would her dad be?

She yanked her gaze from the little girl when Grady broke the oppressive quiet. He stepped forward, holding out his hand. "Pierce, this is a pleasant surprise."

Silvia almost snorted at the word *pleasant*. Maybe Grady thought that, but she didn't. The cobbled-together pieces of her heart didn't, either. They didn't.

"It's good to be back." Pierce's low rumble yanked at the stitches in her heart. There was a time when that voice had melted her as they'd sat in the swing on her parents' porch. When he'd talked for hours about his dreams. When he'd encouraged her in her life goals.

For the past fourteen years, her only memory of him was the cold tone he'd used to tell her he wouldn't wait. Not for her. She should just chase her own dreams, because he was a hometown man, and she was a world-traveling woman. They would never be compatible. The two didn't mix.

Now, he'd traveled the world. And he had a child.

And she didn't.

The air darkened around her. She blinked. Realized Grady was saying something. The other hands were talking and digging into their lunches.

Pierce's voice cut through her fog. "We walked down here for a minute before going to the house. Stretching our legs." His gaze hadn't wavered from her, not even when he'd comforted his daughter. His daughter. Every nerve ending prickled as if she'd been hit by a two-by-four. Had he brought his wife, too? Was he married, and no one had told her? *Please, God, let this floor open up and swallow me.*

Maybe she wanted nothing to do with him anymore. Maybe they were long over. Maybe all her feelings for him had crashed and burned long ago. But seeing him acting lovey-dovey with another woman wasn't on her agenda.

"Excuse me. I have to finish the lunch run." Her tight vocal cords almost mangled the words.

Grady smiled at her and stepped to the side. "Here, Silvia, let me take that for you."

"No, you have your lunch. The wagon isn't heavy." She kept a tight hold on the handle.

Pierce stepped forward, the child lifting her feet and riding along as his leg moved. Just as Silvia had done with her dad when she was young. She pressed her lips into a tight line. *Don't be disarmed by the cuteness and your memories. Just leave.*

"Grady, go ahead with your lunch. I'll help with the wagon. Maybe Kianna would like a ride while we pull it to the car." Pierce broke eye contact to smile down at the child clinging to him. She was so solemn, with an air of sadness. She studied Pierce with so much seriousness, someone might have thought he'd suggested she rewrite the Constitution.

Kianna released him and came over to Silvia holding up her hand. Silvia melted a little. Why was this child so sad? What had happened to her? She took the girl's hand, almost choking at the feel of those small fingers wrapped around hers.

Pierce's hand brushed Silvia's as he tugged on the handle. She tightened her grip as if to say "I can do it myself." But acting like a two-year-old in a power play wasn't a great idea, so she released the wagon, and resigned herself to walking to her car with her ex-boyfriend and his adorable daughter.

Once out the door, Pierce turned to her. "Is it okay if Kianna rides?" At her quick nod, he held out his hands to Kianna, lifting her into the box nestled in the bed of the wagon.

The girl gripped the edges as if they were starting a grand prix race and she was in the lead car.

The gentle smile Pierce gave the girl as he rubbed her back vibrated through Silvia. That smile, the one that said "I've got you," had once been directed at her.

That smile had made her feel safe. Loved.

Not anymore.

"Here we go." Pierce set a slow pace toward her SUV. It was the only vehicle in sight, so he had to know it was hers. Well, her dad's. Maybe he even knew her dad's vehicle. Had he been back home often? Because she hadn't.

"How's your dad?" His question jerked her out of her thoughts. At her uncertain expression, he said, "I heard he had a stroke."

How did the man know everything? "He's better. Have you seen him lately?"

"No, we just got to town. I didn't even know he'd had a stroke until we stopped at Chuckwagon to grab a bite to eat. We've been on the road for the last week, taking our time getting here." He pulled the wagon around to the back and hit the button to open the hatch.

She had a million questions for him. *Are you married? Is your wife here? Why are you here? Where have you been for the last fourteen years?*

Why did you rip my heart to pieces and then have the nerve to come here when I'm home?

He lifted Kianna from the wagon and she ran to hug Silvia as she put the box in the car. Silvia rubbed the girl's back as Pierce had done earlier. Kianna leaned against her.

"You should stop by and see Dad. He'd enjoy the company." She hit the button to close the hatch and stepped toward the driver's door. Would her dad enjoy seeing Pierce?

"I'll do that. I'd like to see him again. It's been a long

time." He shoved his hands in his pockets. "I'm sorry about your mom. She was an amazing lady. Made the best food in the entire country, as far as I'm concerned."

"She was a great cook." Silvia had to concede the point. In all her travels, she'd never met anyone quite like her mom. "And I was sorry to hear about your dad. I hope you got home before he passed."

A pained look tightened his features. He stared off into the distance. "I didn't. I was…overseas at the time."

Silvia softened at the sorrow that filled his eyes. "That's hard. I was out of the country when my mom got sick. It's a hard thing to miss their last days."

Pierce cleared his throat. "I've read some about your adventures." A small smile tipped the corners of his mouth. "Sounds like you did just what you talked about all those years ago."

She swallowed against the tightness in her throat. "Thanks. And it's not over, I'm just back here until my dad is able to take over the restaurant again." She shrugged off the little voice that said he'd never be able to do that. "You always said you'd never leave the ranch, but then you joined the service and traveled all over."

"I did." He lifted Kianna when she left Silvia and held up her hands. "I wanted to prove I would go anywhere, be willing to travel. I'm back now."

Chills raised the hairs on Silvia's arms. Had he done that for her and she hadn't even known? No, surely not. Her gaze dropped to the child. "Will you be staying at the ranch with your mom? I imagine she could use the help."

Pierce frowned. "I'm sure she could. Ranching is hard work. I'm hoping she'll help with Kianna while I take over the majority of the business."

Silvia tilted her head to study him. Just how long had it

been since he'd seen his mom? "I don't think she can care for a child. There are days her disea— Um, she doesn't get out of bed."

His eyes widened, then narrowed. "How do you know that?"

"Because I bring her lunch on those days and stay to visit." Silvia lifted her chin. She sighed, forcing her mixed-up emotions to settle. "Look, if you need help, let me know." With that, she rounded her car, slipped into the driver's seat and drove away.

As Pierce led Kianna across the lawn to the old ranch house where he'd grown up, he kept an eye on the trail of dust billowing behind Silvia's SUV. Seeing her had jolted him back to high school and the first time he'd truly noticed her. Peaches-and-cream complexion. Hair a mix of blond and brown—some called her a straw blonde, and he got the reference from the bales of straw he'd slung on the ranch.

The best part had been when she looked at him back then—truly noticed him for the first time. The way her brown eyes danced and her smile lit up the room. How did one person's smile do that? She'd lit up his heart back then, too. Lit up his whole life. He'd had forever in his sights where Silvia was concerned, but she had different plans. Plans that only included him if he changed his life course, if he gave up his dream of running the ranch.

Part of him regretted not doing that before she left home. Would their lives have been different if he'd made the choice to put her dreams ahead of his?

Silvia had changed. They both had changed, but her eyes no longer danced with joy. And her smile just now had been absent. She carried an air of sadness about her. And the fixer of problems within him wanted to help her. Wanted to bring back the joy she once had. Wanted to see that dazzling smile one more time.

Or maybe more than once.

No one answered his knock at the front door, so he went around to the kitchen door. Kianna leaned against his shoulder. She'd been chattering about meeting her grandmother but must be feeling shy. Had Silvia been correct in what she'd said about his mom? Had her arthritis progressed to the point that she was bedridden part of the time?

He knocked on the kitchen door. The curtain swung aside and his mom peered out at him. Her mouth dropped open, and then she grinned at him. The handle rattled, and he reached out to help turn it since she seemed to be having trouble with it.

Was it even right for him to ask her to take him and Kianna in? Yes, he'd be working to help her, but a child? For the first time, he considered what her rheumatoid arthritis meant with an active little girl around. She'd need help—no, he'd need help.

His thoughts strayed to Silvia. She'd always had a way with kids and a huge heart for those who needed help. Depending on how his mom's illness had progressed, he could put the past behind him and at least ask Silvia for a babysitting recommendation. Someone to come during the day.

"Pierce. You're here." Brenda Forester looked like she'd just stepped out of a magazine photo spread about country homes. Her gray hair swung just above her shoulders. Makeup made her look fresh-faced and sweet. Her pale blue eyes sparkled. Only if he looked close did he notice the dark circles under her eyes and how drawn her face was. "And this must be Kianna!" She reached out to hug Pierce, patting Kianna's arm at the same time.

"This is indeed Kianna. She is in dire need of a break from riding in the car. We both are."

His mom stepped back. "Come on in. I'll put on some fresh coffee."

He nodded, forcing his gaze away from her hands and her twisted fingers. He wouldn't embarrass her by taking away her opportunity to serve. When she made coffee or anything else for him or his siblings, it was an act of love and had been for years. He'd learned all about living with a disability from his mom and her grace in the face of extreme pain.

"Is this our house now?" Kianna held his hand as they made their way to the kitchen table.

"This is my mom's house. We'll be living here, too." At least he hoped so. He'd headed to Arizona with a plan in mind, had let his mom know he wanted to come home for good, but would she believe him? And what would his siblings think? Maybe they didn't want him back here. Maybe his dad's wishes didn't count like they used to. Maybe no one wanted him here.

Well, his mom did. Her greeting left no doubt of that.

"Mom, this smells like more than coffee. Is something cooking?" He led Kianna to the table and helped her into a chair as the microwave dinged.

"It's the middle of the afternoon. I figured you might need a little snack to see you through until dinner." She opened the microwave and reached for a mug with Tinker Bell on it. "Here's a little hot chocolate for Kianna while we have our coffee."

"Let me get that." Pierce took the cup from her and stirred with the spoon she handed him. He tested with his finger and the heat was just right. Trust his mom to know such things. He headed for the table, where Kianna had started bouncing when she heard *hot chocolate*.

"Wait."

He swiveled back to see his mom with one hand on her hip and the other pinching a bag of miniature marshmallows. He grinned, grabbed the bag and took the treat to Kianna.

By the time the marshmallows were added, the buzzer went off on the stove. His mom took two potholders and pulled out a small baking sheet with six fresh cookies on it. Chocolate chip cookies. Her secret recipe. Pierce's mouth watered.

"Mom, when did you make cookie dough?"

She laughed as she placed the cookies on a plate. "You called yesterday. I made up the dough and had it in the refrigerator. I heard your truck earlier and saw you heading to the cookhouse, so I put them in the oven then."

"Perfect timing." He grabbed the two coffee mugs and let her carry the lighter plate. He sat down beside Kianna, who already had a chocolate mustache. Her eyes rounded when she saw the cookies.

When they were all seated at the table with their cookies on napkins, his mom ran a finger around the rim of her mug before using her thumbs and the edges of her knuckles to pick it up and take a drink. Arthritis had twisted her hands until her fingers wouldn't straighten, but she still made the best of it and did all she could do—such as making cookies for a son who hadn't been there for her.

They made small talk while they ate, and then Kianna looked up at him. "Unca Purse?" she mumbled around the last of her cookie. "Can I play?"

Pierce glanced at his mom. What could Kianna play with here? Any toys they'd brought with them were still in the car.

His mom lifted her eyebrows and he nodded. "Of course, honey. Let me show you the toy box." She led Kianna down the hall to a spare room and was soon back. "We always kept a little box of toys in case someone drops by with kids. Need a refresher on your coffee?"

"I'll get it, Mom." Pierce quickly topped off their cooling coffee and sat back down.

"Tell me about Kianna. You wanted to wait to talk in person, but I've been dying to know more." There was no censure in her eyes. No worry. She trusted him to have a reason for showing up with a young child when she knew he'd never married.

"You remember my best friend, Dean Griffin? I brought him home right after we finished our training for Special Forces."

"Of course, I remember. A very nice young man. I don't know why you never brought him around again." She didn't add that he hadn't come home, either.

"Well, Dean married a beautiful woman, Keisha. They asked me to be Kianna's named guardian when she was born." He swallowed hard to ease the tightness in his throat. "Turns out it's my turn to be Kianna's father."

"What happened?" his mom asked.

"We were stationed at the same base. I was babysitting Kianna while Dean and Keisha had a night out. On the way home, a drunk driver plowed into them, killing them both." Pierce cleared his tight throat as the memory of that horror washed over him anew.

Tears glittered in his mom's eyes. Her mouth thinned as she struggled to hold in her emotions. She nodded. Took another sip of coffee. Cleared her throat. "I'm thrilled to have you both here. Are you really here to stay? I didn't want to assume. I understand if you just need a soft place to land for a bit."

The oxygen was sucked from the room. He froze, uncertain what to say. Would his mom really welcome him back to the ranch permanently? Would his brothers and sister? Or were they tired of waiting for him to step up and take his place? Tired of him off fighting somewhere else in the world and never checking in. Tired of him abandoning them.

Time to be a man and face whatever his mom had to say. "Mom, I'm home for good if you'd like. I know Dad wanted me to run the ranch, and I'd like to step up and do that job if you're okay with it. Will it be too much to have Kianna here?"

"Of course, you're both welcome." A tear trickled down her cheek. She touched his arm and he took her hand in both of his, warming her fingers. He felt the tremors run through her and decided he would contact Silvia tonight or tomorrow. No way could he ask his mom to watch Kianna.

"Your father would be so happy. Things have been…" She looked away at the sound of an engine. A vehicle pulled up and stopped, a big truck by the sound of it.

His mom looked back at him. "You remember Chet Mason? He has the ranch a couple miles down the road."

A heavy hand banged on the kitchen door. "Brenda, you home? I've brought the sale papers. Let's get this done."

Chapter Three

"Mom? What papers? What's he talking about?"

Pierce turned as Kianna came running from the spare room to fling herself at him. Since her parents died, Kianna had been very sensitive to loud or harsh voices. He tried to control his tone, but this time he'd slipped. He put his hand on her back and rubbed light circles, breathing easier as she relaxed.

"Brenda. You there?" The loud knocking came again, rattling the door. From where they sat, the person at the door couldn't see them.

Pierce leaned across the table and lowered his voice. "Mom, talk to me."

She nodded. "Just a minute, Chet." She paused as if listening for the rancher's response. Her gaze darted to Kianna. She'd understood the girl's stillness and the meaning from the little he'd shared. His mom tuned into other people like no one else he'd known.

"He's planning to buy the ranch." Tears filled her eyes, and she blinked them away as she lowered her tone to match Pierce's.

"Forester Ranch? Is this something Dad wanted? What about Caleb? Or the twins? What is going on with the ranch?" He snapped his mouth shut. He had no right getting upset. No right to question his mom's decisions. Where had he been when she needed him? Oh, yeah. Hospital. Germany. Wounded. He'd gotten word to his mother that he was safe but recovering from an injury, had asked her not to share it with anyone else, even his siblings. He couldn't share with his family what he did in the military. The rescue missions he'd been involved in were top secret. After that last bullet and surgery—combined with losing Dean and becoming Kianna's guardian—he'd decided to take the medical discharge offered.

"I'm on my own here." She shrugged, not meeting his eyes. "Since your dad died, I can't keep it up. Grady stepped in as temporary foreman. But I need someone to help with decisions and figuring out what direction the ranch should take. We aren't making money, or not much." She hiccupped a sob, eyes luminous with unshed tears. "I just can't do what I used to do."

This ranch had been his great-great-grandfather's, passed down through the family. They had grazing rights that had been grandfathered in. His dad had been so proud of this land, some of the most beautiful in the area. He'd worked hard, taught his children what it meant to be a Forester and to carry on their legacy.

And they'd all let him down. Let their mom down.

Would his being here be too little, too late? He'd had hints in the last few months that the ranch wasn't on an even keel but he didn't know times were so desperate. Maybe he should let this sale go through. Take his mom and Kianna somewhere else and start over fresh.

Son, this land is in our blood. We have a heritage to be proud of, not just our spiritual heritage, but this land given us by God. We have to work hard to care for His gift.

How many times had his father told him that? Passed on tales of his ancestors and their fight for this place and how they wanted to provide for the generations after them. No way could he stand by and let Chet Mason, or anyone else, have this land. He'd come home to help. Maybe he'd come home to a fight. If so, he was a Special Forces soldier who knew how to plan strategy and fight a war.

"Mom." He took her hands in his. Held them until she looked at him. "I'm here to help, and I plan to stay. I left the army. Send Chet on his way, and let's talk about what we can do."

A flicker of something shone in her eyes. Hope? Relief? She gave a quick nod and rose from the table.

He patted Kianna's back and kissed her temple. "It's okay. Go on back and play while your grandma and I talk to the man outside." At the mention of returning to the toys, her eyes lit up. She slid off his lap and trotted back down the hall. He stood and followed his mom to the door, twisted the handle and pulled it open for her.

Chet Mason stood at the base of the step, a folder in his hand. A Stetson shadowed his thin face. Eyes that missed nothing darted from Pierce's mom to Pierce and back.

"Brenda." He nodded and removed his hat. "Mind if I come in? I drew up our agreement and have it ready for you to sign." He lifted the folder.

"Your agreement?" Pierce held out a hand for the folder, but Chet didn't hand it over. "You didn't go through a mortgage company?"

"We're neighbors. We look out for one another." Chet's eyes hardened as he stared at Pierce. "Pierce." He nodded. "Your mom and I worked out the terms on our own."

"Things have changed, Chet. I'm sorry. I'll need more time since I have company." Mom's voice wavered. Her hands trembled where she held on to the door. "Maybe we can talk again in a couple of weeks."

"I see." Chet frowned. "We had an agreement, Brenda. A

verbal agreement. In these parts, that's as good as a signature on paper. I'll give you that time, but I expect you to sign these papers. I've been generous to your crew and to you. There's an allowance for you to have time to vacate the premises." He slammed his hat back on his head and turned toward where he'd parked his truck.

Pierce held still, stuffing down the anger so he wouldn't upset Kianna or his mom. "Chet." He waited until the man turned back to face him. "Leave the papers here for Mom to look over."

The rancher's jaw flexed as he glared at Pierce. Finally, he came back and handed the folder to Brenda. "One week."

"Two weeks," Pierce said with a growl.

"Fine. Be prepared to sign."

Pierce stepped to the side to let his mom go back to the kitchen. He stayed in the doorway and watched as Chet got in his truck, turned it around and gunned it down the driveway, bouncing through the ruts like he didn't care about damage to the suspension.

Talk about getting home in the nick of time. One more day and he might not have had a ranch to come back to. He felt a flash of guilt. Had all of the Forester children left the ranch? Quinn and Ashlyn had moved to LA for some TV show. Their hearts had never been with this land. But Caleb's had. He'd thought his youngest brother was here, helping out. Why did his mom think she was on her own?

He closed the door and turned back to the kitchen table. His mom set the folder by his now cool cup of coffee before sitting down again.

Pierce settled in and opened the sheaf of papers to see what Chet thought was a good deal. The more he read, the angrier he got. Chet Mason had always been a man with an agenda— to be the most important person around. He claimed to know important people and often took over smaller ranches when the owners couldn't make a profit in tough times.

But the offer he'd put on paper for the Forester Ranch was highway robbery. Sure, his mom might end up with enough extra to get a small house in town and live comfortably for a while. But this ranch and the grazing rights were worth at least ten times what Chet offered. No wonder he didn't want to go through a mortgage office. They would never have allowed this.

Even the amount he offered for the livestock was pitiful. They had purebred stock, sought after all over the country. A few cows were worth more than Chet offered for the entire herd.

Now, to convince his mom he'd truly come home to help her. And maybe talk about enlisting help—like Silvia's since she offered. Even if just for suggesting where he could hire help.

By the time she reached the Chuckwagon restaurant, Silvia wanted to be done with the day. To take a blistering hot shower, grab a cup of chai and settle in with a good book. To forget this day had ever happened.

To forget about seeing Pierce.

She left the wagon in the car but carried the empty boxes in through the back door. The noon rush was long over and Jeanne and her helpers were prepping for the dinner rush. September meant that the end-of-summer influx of campers looking for a meal not cooked over a campfire and tourists passing through had slowed to a trickle. But there were still plenty of locals who appreciated a good meal, and Chuckwagon provided wholesome food that stuck with the customers.

Maybe the food had stuck with her too much. Her jeans

seemed a tad tighter now than they'd been when she arrived. Of course, she ate and worked instead of spending hours curled in a fetal position, staring at a picture of her son.

"Silvia, you've had some calls today." Jeanne fast-walked over to her from the counters. "That fancy agent of yours called and demanded you call her back. Some editor also called. Catherine something."

Silvia nodded. She had to quit avoiding their calls and face working on the book she and Keith had been so excited about writing. "Anyone else?"

"One of the suppliers. Some problem with the order. I left a note on the desk. Let me know if you need help sorting it out." Jeanne squeezed her arm, grabbed the boxes and shoved them under a workstation, to be filled the next morning.

The cook swung back around. "Oh, and Meena called in sick. She won't be able to work tonight." Meena was one of the high school girls who worked evenings and was saving money for college.

"I hope it's nothing serious." Silvia would need to call someone to take the girl's place.

Jeanne leaned close and lowered her voice. "My guess is her sickness has to do with the game tonight. It's a junior varsity game and her twin brothers are playing. Plus, there's probably a chance she'll see that Norton boy she's been dating."

"I'll find someone to fill in." Silvia headed for the office, not wanting to be drawn into small-town drama. Around here, everyone knew everyone else's business. It could be a comfort, but most times she found it annoying. Always had. Especially when she'd been in high school and people considered it their duty to call her parents and tell them what she'd been caught doing. Her parents hadn't been authoritarian, but still.

She sat at the desk, opened her laptop and pulled up the

list of employees to see who might sub for Meena. They had two other high school girls who always liked extra hours, but if this was a game night, they might not be interested. She considered calling Tilly, another high school part-timer. She wasn't in to socializing, and with her family situation she needed the money that extra hours would provide.

Knowing the girl would be in class, Silvia sent a quick text to see if she was interested in filling the spot. She hadn't even set down the phone when Tilly sent back a resounding yes. She would be at the restaurant by four to help with setup for the dinner rush and then serve until closing.

One down, three calls to make. She fingered the notes Jeanne had left on the desk. Glanced at the book folder on her laptop that seemed to mock her.

She was so thankful that she'd been in the habit of scheduling blog posts months in advance for when she and Keith were away from the internet. Plus, Marissa, her agent had helped with the social media side, posting that Silvia was dealing with a family issue. A family issue.

She closed her eyes against the wave of dizziness that spun through her head. That moment of excitement for Keith and Steven as they soared overhead. The moment that turned from elation to horror as they tumbled from the sky. The fall that followed. And the agony of loss that she still endured.

She opened her eyes to see tears splashing on the desktop. She grabbed a tissue to wipe them up and swiped at her face. *It's been a year. Stop crying.*

But when you've lost everything, there is so much to cry about.

The picture of Pierce and his adorable little girl standing by her car hurt too. She wondered what had happened to Kianna's family. According to Jeanne, who always seemed to know everything, she wasn't Peirce's biological child but rather an orphan he'd adopted. To be a child and suffer such grief must be overwhelming. Maybe that's why she clung to Pierce, why she had that lost look in her eyes. Silvia's heart went out to the little girl. If she had the chance, she'd do everything possible to make Kianna feel welcome and loved.

Pierce was another story. She'd be polite, but keeping her distance was a must. An absolute must. Because her reaction to him today told her that while she may have moved on in life, she hadn't forgotten her first love.

Not at all.

When the phone buzzed, she reached for it. The supplier. She spent the next twenty minutes going over their order, discussing the shortages at the company and choosing replacement items that should work.

Next, she called her agent in New York. Listened to her firm admonishments about delayed deadlines and editorial expectations. Promised to get back to work on the book. Talked about how to get in the last few adventures for the final three chapters needed. By the time she hung up, she'd run out of energy—mental energy, anyway. At least her agent promised to talk with the editor, so that was one call she didn't have to make.

Before, the thought of going on another adventure had always filled her with so much excitement that she had trouble sitting still on the plane when they traveled. Now, the thought of doing this without Keith and Steven left her dry as dust. She didn't know how to get back her enthusiasm.

The restaurant phone rang again before she'd completed the bookwork. "Chuckwagon. How may I help you?"

"Silvia?"

Her heart gave a thump. Pierce. She recognized his voice as if they'd only spoken on the phone yesterday. "Yes, Pierce. How can I help you?" She allowed a tinge of frost in her tone.

He sighed. "Look, Silvia, I know I hurt you but I need help and you're the only one I really know. Plus, Kianna likes you."

"What kind of help?" She wasn't touching his admission of having hurt her.

"You were right. My mom's health isn't great." He paused and cleared his throat. "I know you're busy with the restaurant but I can't saddle Mom with Kianna's care. Would you be able to help out? I'm not asking you to do anything, just give me suggestions for child care."

"Are you looking for someone to come to the ranch?"

"Once I get her set up in school, I need someone to help take her and pick her up on the days when I have to work with the cattle. Someone who could watch her until late afternoon or evening." He sounded like he was holding his breath waiting for her answer.

I can do it. Her fast answer should be no. She didn't want to be around Pierce. But the fact was they lived in a small rural area and she couldn't escape meeting up with him. Plus, the sadness on that little girl's face, and the way Kianna had clung to her at the ranch earlier, tugged at her heart. She sighed. "I don't know anyone, but perhaps I can help. Maybe you can text me your schedule." At least with a text she wouldn't have to see him in person.

By the time she'd finished the bookwork, checked with Jeanne, who was ready to leave, and noted that Tilly was on the job, she'd almost run out of energy to even walk out the back door to her car. She grabbed meals to take home for their dinner and drove through the Ashville evening traffic. In most cities, this wouldn't be worth calling traffic.

"I'm home." She set the dinners on the counter and hung her sweater on the rack by the door. September evenings in the mountains ranged from brisk to downright cold.

"Come look," her father called from the front room. She

went down the hall to see him standing by the side window overlooking the field just west of the house. She stopped beside him and cupped her hand around his arm, noting his slight tremors.

In the gathering dusk, a herd of elk grazed their way through the field. They were so majestic and graceful. The bull elk had a rack that most hunters would...well, kill for. But she preferred to see the antlers on the elk, not eat the animal.

"How's the Chuckwagon? Get the l-l-lunches delivered?"

She debated telling him about seeing Pierce, but her dad hadn't been happy about their breakup all those years ago. *Why did I suggest Pierce stop by?* Instead, she related a couple of stories from other ranchers that had him smiling. He missed seeing his friends and interacting with people at the restaurant. She understood.

"Ready for dinner, Dad? I can heat the lasagna I brought. You know Jeanne's is the best." She'd had trouble getting him to eat since his stroke. Chewing was harder for him, but he was managing and getting better. He was back on regular food now, although she tried to only bring him softer foods.

"In a minute. I want to watch these elk." He stared out at the large bull for a few minutes while she stood beside him.

"Silvia."

She looked up to find him watching her instead of the herd, his expression solemn. "Yes."

"I don't think I'll ever come back. To the restaurant."

She squeezed his arm. "Dad, give it time."

As she walked into the kitchen, her phone buzzed. An unknown number. "Hello?"

"Silvia, thank you for answering." Evident relief sounded in Pierce's voice. Her heart thumped as memories of hours spent on the phone with him flooded through her.

"How did you get my number?"

"From my mom." He hesitated. "I just wanted to thank you for agreeing to help and for the heads-up about my mom."

"How is she?" She leaned back against the counter, dinner forgotten.

"You were right." He sighed. "I didn't realize how much Mom's disease has progressed. She overextended today and is in bed now. She even admitted she won't be able to help most days. Did you mean what you said? Will you help me with Kianna?"

She closed her eyes, picturing the amber-eyed little girl with her off-kilter ponytail and the weight of the world on her shoulders. "Yes, I'll help when I can."

"Thank you. Thank you." She heard Pierce swallow. "I'll be in town tomorrow to talk to the school. I can come by the Chuckwagon to talk with you if that's okay."

Chapter Four

Five days. Five days since Chet Mason had given his ultimatum, and Pierce was no closer to figuring out the ranch business than when he started. First, the books were a mess. Not to mention the livestock records. Must-do items for the fall were behind. It was past time to get the cattle down from the high pastures, although Grady was working on that.

Add to that a whirlwind day of meetings with the school administrator and counselor followed by school-supply shopping with Kianna. Pierce was grateful he'd been able to get her enrolled in afternoon kindergarten on short notice. That fit perfectly with the times Silvia could pick her up.

He'd spent the rest of the week digging through the ranch's files. And he still had no idea what had put the ranch on a borderline loss of revenue. He stood and stretched his aching limbs. Sitting for long hours wasn't his thing. He'd been as restless as a caged cat last night, not even able to settle down for Kianna when she wanted to watch a princess movie.

The only bright spot was the way Silvia had stepped in to help with Kianna, picking her up from school and bringing her home at dinnertime on Thursday and Friday. Just the thought of her lifted some of the load he carried.

Although he did wonder… When Silvia had dropped her off Friday afternoon, his daughter had flung her arms around Silvia's leg. She was already a big fan of "Ms. Silvia," it seemed, but when Silvia had glanced down at the girl, something flashed across her face. Pain? Sorrow? He hadn't kept up with her much at all after she married. He'd had too much going on in his own life with the team and missions and missing his home with an ache that never left. What had happened to Silvia?

A knock sounded on the office door. "Come in." He turned from staring out the window and realized the time. Lunchtime. There was a surcharge for Saturday deliveries, but it was one worth paying for, in Pierce's opinion. In just a few days, his inner timer had reset to go off when it was time for Silvia to deliver lunches for the crew.

He might not admit it to anyone, but his heart had never forgotten Silvia. Her love of life still shone through as she interacted with his crew. For them, she laughed, although she was not as carefree as she used to be. And while she'd been lovely with Kianna, she'd seemed closed off with him, a shell of herself.

"Pierce? You okay?"

His mom must have been talking while he was lost in thought. "I'm good. How can I help you? Does Kianna need something?"

"No, that child is a treasure." His mom's soft smile warmed him. His mom was having a good day and wanted to watch his daughter. "She's a rather sad treasure, but I think she'll be just fine. A loving home can work wonders."

"That it can." He shut the lid on his laptop.

"Are you ready for lunch? Kianna helped fix the food and is pretty proud of her table-setting skills."

He laughed. "I can't wait to see." The first time Kianna set the table, she only gave them spoons to eat with. If they'd had soup, that would have worked, but with spaghetti they needed something to pick up the noodles. He and his mom waited for

Kianna to realize this, and then sent her to the kitchen for the forks. Lesson learned, and she hadn't been upset.

"Something smells good in here." He drew in a deep breath and his stomach growled as he entered the kitchen. Kianna covered her mouth with her hand and giggled, the best sound he'd heard in weeks.

He picked her up and gave her a hug. "I hear you've been cooking. I hope I don't have to eat cat food."

"Unca Purse." Kianna giggled again. "I didn't make cat food."

"Then what did you make? Or maybe I'll just eat you up." He made growling noises and pretended to gnaw on her neck. She squealed and wiggled in his arms. He set her down, and she took his hand.

"Sit down, Unca Purse." She led him to the dining table, and he found a coloring page and crayons at his place. Yes, he had been restless last night at dinner. She must have equated that with kids needing a distraction at a restaurant. Today, he was her kid at the table.

He sat down and glanced at his mom, who was biting her lip, trying not to laugh. When Kianna headed back to the kitchen, Pierce grinned at Mom and picked out a crayon.

They had grilled cheese sandwiches and apple slices. The sandwiches were his favorite, with three kinds of cheese and toasted to perfection. His mom hadn't lost her touch. And she remembered his favorites from his youth.

"Ladies, that was the best meal yet." He wiped his mouth and put his napkin on his plate.

"Wait." Kianna spoke with her mouth full. At his look, she chewed fast and spoke around her bite. "We made bwownies. With candy in them." Her eyes sparkled more than he'd seen since her parents died.

He plucked his napkin from the plate and smoothed it

over his lap. "In that case, I'm staying here. Bring on the brownies."

The brownies not only had M&M's, but also a ribbon of caramel running through them. Delicious. Another old favorite.

"Kianna and I have been talking. We'd like to do some shopping this afternoon if you have the time to take us to town." His mom gathered the plates and stacked them. He took them from her and carried them to the kitchen.

"Mom, I have to keep working on the books and figuring out the ranch. If we want to save it from Chet Mason, I need to see what's been going wrong. I only have a week and a bit left."

"I know." She put her hand on his arm. "I also wanted to give you Donald Norton's card. He's our lawyer, and I know you want to talk to him about the ranch."

"Did you consult him about the sale?"

"I mentioned it to him, but we didn't discuss any of the particulars." She didn't meet his gaze, and looked off toward the dining area. Kianna had retrieved the coloring page and crayons, and was finishing the picture.

"What did he say?" Pierce covered her hand with his.

"He may have suggested I not sell. That I hire a competent manager instead." She looked at him this time. "Thing is, I know nothing about ranch managers. I wouldn't know a good one from a bad one. And I just didn't have the energy to try. But maybe Donald can explain his reasoning."

"That's a good idea. I'll run it by Grady first and see what he says. Then I'll have two opinions besides what I learned in school."

His mom frowned. "In school?"

He rolled his shoulders. There was a lot his mom didn't know about him or his life while he'd been gone. "I took college classes in the service. Most of them were online and my professors understood if I was on deployment that my lessons might be turned in late. I ended up with a degree in agriculture management."

Her mouth dropped open. Her eyes lit up. "Pierce, I'm so proud of you. Did you always mean to come back here?"

"I never meant to leave. It just happened." He had no way to explain why he'd joined the service and left his family in the lurch.

"That's okay. You're here now. Go talk to Grady, and I'll get us ready to go."

He strode across to the cookhouse just as Silvia was exiting, pulling her little wagon behind her. She was wearing a flowing blue top today and her hair hung in a braid over her left shoulder, almost to her waist. She smiled over her shoulder at something someone said and then turned and caught sight of him.

He stopped, unable to do anything but watch her. She froze, staring at him. They were caught in that moment. He fumbled with what to say. Why did seeing her turn his brain to mush? "Hey, Silvia."

Since the first day Pierce had shown up, Silvia dreaded these moments. Seeing him again. Being caught in the laser beam of his eyes. Remembering all the ways they once fit together. How they could never fit together again.

"Morning." She nodded at him, hoping that would be enough. Tugged on the wagon handle. Willed her feet to move.

"It's not." His low, rumbly voice stopped her in her tracks. *It's not?* What did that mean? Was something wrong with his mom? Kianna? And why did she even care? The man had stomped all over her heart, so let him have a terrible morning.

Except that wasn't her. She cared too much about people.

How many times had she and Keith used their days off to work for some charity organization in need of help in whatever country they were in at the time? She'd always loved making children smile when they had no reason to be happy. To see those faces light up with joy. To sing wordless songs with them or dance in a circle just for the sheer joy of being alive and having someone who cared.

She straightened her shoulders. "Why is it such an awful morning?" She glanced toward the house.

He chuckled. "It isn't morning. That's all I meant." He lifted his arm and tapped his bare wrist as if there was a watch there. "It's officially afternoon." The edges of his mouth tipped up, and he crossed his arms over his chest.

She snorted. He'd always been so exacting, while she had a more low-key view of life. They'd balanced one another, a fact she'd forgotten, or repressed in the dark recesses of her mind. She and Keith had been on the same page. They'd found a rhythm in their life, one she enjoyed. But they'd never had that spark she'd had with Pierce. She didn't need sparks anymore. That was for young people.

"Well, afternoon then." She nodded and tugged the wagon as she set off for her SUV. The rattle and bump of the wheels on the uneven ground precluded conversation. Maybe he would continue on to the cookhouse while she scooted down the road. A simple greeting to a neighbor or client, that was all.

She hit the button and the rear hatch slid up. She grabbed the box and put it in the back. Strong hands lifted the wagon, and she turned to find Pierce waiting for her to step aside. She did, and he slid the wagon into its spot.

"Thank you. I can do that, you know." She didn't mean to sound testy. Maybe he hadn't heard it that way. It was just that having him this close set off alarms she hadn't realized were still in place. *Dad, get well faster. Lord, keep me on track with Your plan.*

"I wanted to thank you again for agreeing to help with Kianna in the afternoons. I don't know what I'd do without you."

Silvia waved her hand. "She's a gem. I don't mind at all."

He pushed the button, and the hatch lowered at turtle speed. A flash of color caught her eye. His charge, running across the lawn, her caramel-colored braids bouncing on her shoulders. She was just too cute.

"Unca Purse. Miss Silvy."

Pierce turned. A grin lit his face. That grin used to warm her from the inside out when he turned it on her. He loved this little girl. He swooped her up in his arms when she leaped the last two feet and caught her to his chest. Kianna slapped her hands on his cheeks and pressed her nose to his. Silvia almost melted into a puddle on the ground. She'd always been a sucker for dads who loved their kids. Seeing Pierce love a little girl who wasn't his biologically meant even more.

"What's up, sweetie?" He kissed her forehead before rearing back to study her face. "Is Grandma needing help?"

"Nope. She said I had 'nurgee and needed to run like a coat."

Silvia covered her mouth to hold back a snort. Pierce compressed his lips, his gaze darting to her and then back to Kianna.

"Maybe Grandma said you had too much energy and needed to run like a colt. Is that it?"

Kianna nodded vigorously, her braids almost hitting Pierce in the chin. "Yes, that's what I said."

"Okay, Grandma knows these things. You see that corral there?" He pointed toward the barn. "That's called a lunging ring. We take the colts in there and have them gallop or run in circles. Sounds like Grandma wants you to run around there. Can you do that? Just slide through the fence and gallop around." She nodded again and pushed against his chest. He set her down, and she was off.

Silvia swiped at her eyes and allowed some of her laughter out. She gasped and glanced at Pierce. He grinned at her. She shook her head. "She's a hoot. How long before she realizes what a colt is and that she's not one?"

He laughed. "I'm hoping for a few years." His expression grew thoughtful. "I'm just glad to see her laughing. The entire trip here, she was so solemn I didn't think I'd ever see her smile again. I had trouble getting her to eat or sleep."

"And here, it's different." Silvia's eyes burned as she watched the little girl run circles with abandon. She wanted to ask how long it had been since her parents died, but that might be too personal. She and Pierce were no longer friends. And she needed to get back on the road with her deliveries.

She rounded the SUV, opened the door, paused and peered at him over the roof. "I keep meaning to ask—why does she call you Uncle Purse?"

His face flushed a ruddy color. "They were among her first words. Keisha thought it was so cute that she never corrected her. She's always called me Uncle Purse. Maybe someday she'll realize that's not accurate."

"When she's older, she can call you Uncle Gucci." She grinned as he rolled his eyes, and she slipped into the vehicle. As Pierce headed for the corral, she backed up and eased down the rutted lane, her thoughts filled with a young girl, orphaned, and how blessed that child was to have Pierce as her guardian.

By the time she got home that night, her feet hurt and she wanted nothing more than a hot shower and to fall into bed. But she needed to work with her dad. The home health worker had called her to discuss some things she could do to help him with recovery. She had a plan and needed to implement that. Her father's stroke had been mild compared to many. He already had most of his movement and speech back, but he needed work to smooth things out.

"Hey, Dad." She heard the television click off as she called out. He only watched TV during the day, when he was bored. "Want to help me with dinner?" She put her keys in the dish on the entry table and slid her purse underneath. Kianna calling Pierce "Unca Purse" flitted through her mind and she almost laughed out loud.

She stopped at the entrance to the living room, the bag of supplies in her arms. "I brought supper in kit form. I thought we could cook together like we used to. You know, me working and you bossing me around." She winked at her dad and he smiled with only a slight droop to the left side of his mouth.

For the next thirty minutes, she buzzed around the kitchen, assembling most of the meal, while he stirred the sauce for pasta. She told him about Pierce and Kianna, and he chuckled over the story with the corral.

As they ate, she carried the bulk of the conversation but asked questions and waited patiently for the answer. Chrissy, the home health-care nurse, explained that his brain might be slower to come up with answers, especially in the evening, but if she gave him time, he'd get there. And she was right.

"Why is Pierce back?" His question caught her off guard. What did she say? She hadn't asked. Had been afraid to ask.

"I don't know. Maybe he's on leave." Even as she said that, it rang false. Sure, they hadn't talked much about his plans, but he had mentioned running the ranch for his mom. He wouldn't do that if he was still an enlisted soldier.

Chapter Five

Why is Pierce back? Her dad's question had rattled around in her head the past two days, along with all her confusing emotions concerning the man she once loved. Somewhere deep down, she still cared for him. And she adored his daughter. Silvia had picked her up Thursday and Friday last week, and then again yesterday. Now, it was Tuesday, a Pierce day, and she found herself missing the little girl. They'd already had so much fun spending time together.

She climbed from her car, where she'd been sitting as the early morning chill chased away remnants of heat, lost in a daze of thought. She grabbed her purse, aware she'd been running behind all morning. Getting her dad settled had taken longer than usual. She'd spilled cereal milk all down her front and had to change clothes. One thing after another went wrong, and her mental fog from lack of sleep didn't help.

"You've got this. Bake cookies. Make sandwiches. Pack box lunches. Do the deliveries." She paused, her hand on the back door, taking a deep breath of pine-scented air. "Get the work done and maybe grab a nap in the office."

A girl could dream, couldn't she?

The kitchen was already busy. The restaurant opened at six in the morning, and it was almost seven. Late, late, late. She hurried to stash her purse in the office and pull on an apron.

"Morning, Silvia," Jeanne called from across the kitchen.

"I got here early and mixed up cookie dough. It's labeled in the cold box. All you have to do is bake them."

"Thank you." Silvia hoped her simple reply conveyed the depth of her gratitude. After all that had gone wrong, this one simple gift felt huge and boosted her flagging spirits.

An hour later, she had all the cookies baked and carried some out to the dining room to put on display, keeping back what she'd need for the lunches. And one to take home for her dad—cranberry-orange with white chocolate chips. His favorite.

The bell over the door dinged as she straightened from adding the last of the cookies to the shelves of baked goods. Pierce and Kianna stood there, looking for a spot to sit. When his gaze found her, she froze. Somehow, one look from Pierce seemed like a full-on hug. What was it about this man?

"Miss Silvy." Kianna bounced on her toes and gave a small wave. Silvia had to smile. This morning the little girl was wearing a pair of jeans, a flannel shirt and a brand-new pair of cowgirl boots.

Silvia stepped around the counter. She bent down to Kianna's level, ignoring the pull of Pierce. "Looks like someone did some shopping. Don't you look nice?"

"I gots boots." Kianna lifted one foot in the air. "Pink ones."

"Those are definitely pink. And sparkly." Silvia glanced up at Pierce and tried not to laugh at his pained look. Evidently, sparkly pink wasn't his idea.

She gave Kianna a hug. "Are you here for some breakfast?"

"Yes." The little girl pointed to the display case. "I want cookies and milk for breakfast."

Pierce gave an exaggerated sigh. "You can't have cookies and milk for breakfast. Remember?"

Kianna's lower lip protruded. "But there's cookie cereal

and you add milk to it. Betina had it at her house and we ate some."

"That's different. That cereal has nutrition in it, too." Pierce grimaced at Silvia, as if he realized the shaky ground he stood on.

"Cookies don't have 'trition?"

Silvia chuckled and decided to help. "My dad used to say I had to eat my eggs or pancakes and then I could have a cookie. Maybe your uncle will agree to that."

Kianna put her hands together under her chin in a praying position and gazed up at Pierce with big eyes. Oh, boy. This girl already knew how to bend this man around her little finger. Silvia bit her lip to keep from laughing out loud.

"I want canpakes." Kianna blinked her wide eyes again.

Pierce chuckled, and Silvia grinned. She stood up. "Why don't you grab that booth over there? The server will be there in a minute." She headed back to the kitchen with her cookie tray and put it in the stack of dishes to be washed, then checked the cookies.

While they cooled, she pulled out the list of box lunches for today. Each cowboy put in his order from a limited menu. Today's options were roast beef or turkey sandwich, apple or chips, and either a peanut-butter or cranberry-orange cookie, and they got a choice of soda or juice to drink.

Her dad had had a good idea with this service. To be part of the program, the ranches had to be within a certain driving range, which was much different here than in a city. When doing deliveries, she started with the farthest, fifty-five miles away, and worked her way back. Her route actually ran in a loop that included Concho and St. Johns, two small towns in Northern Arizona. So far, they had five ranches using their lunch-delivery service, but a couple more east of here had contacted her and shown interest. If they signed on, the restaurant would need an extra driver for that route.

Darcy, their only waitress this morning, came into the kitchen looking a little tired. "Silvia, I know this isn't my break time, but I need a few minutes." She looked pale and held her hand on her stomach.

"Go. I've got the customers." Silvia wiped her hands, covered the food she had put out and headed for the dining room. The early breakfast crowd had thinned out. There were a few tables of regulars who liked to eat, drink lots of coffee and chat with their friends. She removed empty plates, filled cups and then saw Pierce and Kianna still at their table. She wandered over with the coffeepot.

"Need a refill?"

Pierce pushed his half-empty mug in her direction, and she poured fresh coffee in the cup. Kianna was busy coloring, her pancake mostly eaten and a little stickiness still on her cheek.

"How were the pancakes, Kianna?"

"They were yummy. With chocolate chips." She frowned. "But Unca Purse says I already had enough sugar and can't have a cookie. I didn't even eat any sugar." Tears glittered in her eyes. Silvia repressed a snort.

"Your uncle is probably right. Did you know pancake syrup is made of sugar? That's why it's so sticky." She smoothed a curl that had sprung free from Kianna's pigtail.

"I have to see our lawyer, Donald Norton. I don't think having a girl with a sugar high along is a good idea." Pierce shook his head at his daughter's crestfallen expression. "How about we come back and buy a cookie afterward to eat on the way home? We can share one, because you know your grandma is always baking something."

"Okay." Kianna bounced and clapped, then returned to her coloring.

"You're taking a child hyped up on syrup to a dull lawyer meeting?"

"Glutton for punishment. He wasn't available yesterday, and Kianna has a day off from school." He shook his head. "Mom's not having a good day today, and I can't put this meeting off any further."

"Let her stay here. I'll put her to work." Silvia shrugged at Pierce's grateful look.

"But this isn't a time we agreed to." Pierce stared at Silvia, ignoring the excited interest that had Kianna bouncing again on the overstuffed booth seat. "This is my day to watch her." He didn't want to say anything to hurt Kianna. For the first time in weeks, she'd come out of her shell, and he'd do anything to keep her on the right track. She loved being here with Silvia.

"She can help me pack lunches for delivery. Besides, she's my chef's assistant on the afternoons I've had her. Right Kianna?"

She smiled down at Kianna, who nodded enthusiastically. "Can I wear my special gloves?" Pierce had heard all about the kid-size gloves Kianna wore when she was in the restaurant kitchen after school.

"You bet. Think you can put cookies in baggies? I'll show you how and be right there to help. Then you can tell Grady and the other cowboys how you helped make their lunches."

"I'm a good helper." Kianna clapped her hands. "My mommy always said so." Pierce's throat constricted as Kianna froze. This was the first time she'd mentioned either of her parents other than asking for them in those first days or crying for them in the middle of the night. He wasn't sure she remembered those times, but he sure did.

"What do you think, Uncle Purse?" Silvia's eyes twinkled

as her lips quirked up at the corners. She used to give him that look when she knew she'd gotten the better of him. She always made him laugh. He missed those days with a soul-deep ache.

"I shouldn't be too long. I guess it would be okay, if you're sure." He dug some bills from his pocket to pay the check.

"Thank you." Kianna bounced clear off the seat. Silvia grabbed her before she hit the floor and didn't even spill any of the coffee in the pot she held.

"Kianna." He held his arms open for a hug. Gave her a quick kiss on the temple. "Remember, you're here to help bag the cookies, not eat them." He chuckled at her outraged look, hugged her tight and set her down.

He stood. Touched Silvia's arm, the contact reverberating up his arm. "I'll try to hurry." Silvia waved him off and took Kianna by the hand to lead her to the kitchen as the Darcy hurried back into the room, tying her apron around her waist. Silvia spoke to her for a moment before disappearing into the kitchen.

Pierce held the door for an older couple that he might have known years ago. They looked familiar, but the names escaped him.

The morning had warmed up. The sun felt good on his face and the fresh air had him breathing deep. Across the street, a herd of horses grazed in a field. He had yet to take Kianna riding, but it was on the list of things to do. She already loved going out to watch the cowboys ride off, or to see them working with the cattle. Everything here was so different from her life back east. Quite the adjustment on top of being an orphan. *Please, Lord, help me know how to be a dad to Kianna. Show me Your will for the ranch, too.*

Donald Norton had a small office just off Main Street. He'd turned an old cottage into a nice practice. He only had office hours two mornings a week here. The rest of the time, he went to the Show Low-Pinetop area, where he had another office that was probably more lucrative since Ashville was so small.

"Pierce Forester." Norton came around his desk as the receptionist showed him into the office. Donald Norton spent too much time behind a desk or eating with his clients. His neatly trimmed beard hid some of the softness of his face. The white beard contrasted with his darker hair. His grin was warm and welcoming, though.

"I remember when you were the star at Ashville High. We thought you'd go places in college or for some team. I remember you being pretty good at baseball. What have you been doing?" Norton gestured to a set of chairs and they settled in. Pierce appreciated that the man didn't feel the need to sit behind his desk.

"I've been in the army."

"The army? With your talent. What happened with the scouts? I know they were looking at you."

Small towns. You had to love the people who cared, even when they wanted to know every detail of your life. "I got a couple of offers. I chose to go into the military instead."

"A man's gotta make a choice about his life. Has the military been good to you?" Norton lifted one ankle to put on his other knee.

"Very good. Thank you."

"So how can I help you, Pierce? I'm sorry about your dad. He was a fine man."

"Thank you. I understand you worked with him or advised him on ranch business." Pierce told Norton about the incident with Chet Mason and pulled out the contract the man had given his mom. He waited while Norton read through the papers.

"You say he gave her two weeks? That he thinks he can make her sign this?"

"Yes, and it's taken me a week to sort it all out as much as I have so far. He seems to think the offer represents a valid price for the land and the cattle, including the grazing rights."

Donald drew in a deep breath and tapped the papers with his finger. "This offer is laughable. I know your dad sold off some of the livestock to help with expenses, but he still had plenty of stock left. That was a couple of years ago, so his herd should have built up from then. He talked to me about his plan."

"The thing is, I'm having trouble finding his plan. The paperwork is a mess and sorting through it is taking more time than I expected. Dad used to be meticulous with everything, but Mom says he slipped in the months before he died."

"The last couple of times I spoke with your dad, I was concerned about his health. He assured me he was seeing a doctor, but he wasn't as sharp as he used to be."

"Do you have a copy of the plan you discussed with him? And what do you think about Chet's claim that Mom has to sell to him?"

They spent the rest of the hour mapping out a strategy and looking over the papers his dad left with Norton. By the time they finished, the tension in Pierce's neck had eased.

"Thank you for your help." He shook the lawyer's hand and walked back out into the sunshine. He hoped Kianna hadn't run Silvia and everyone else at the restaurant ragged. He had this image of his daughter taking a bite out of every cookie before she bagged it up. Sounded like something he might have done at her age.

The Chuckwagon had emptied some. It was past the breakfast hour and not yet time for the lunch rush. Pierce wanted to get home and run some of his ideas by Grady. Turned out his dad was training Grady be the ranch foreman, but hadn't implemented that before he died. Pierce intended to rectify that, or at least make Grady his assistant in training. They could work together and bring the ranch back to what it had once been.

Chet Mason had no claim on the land or the cattle. None.

Jeanne peered out through the window from the kitchen. She waved to Pierce and indicated he should come on back. He pushed open the kitchen door to the cutest sight he'd seen in a long time.

Silvia stood on the far side of a long table, filling lunch boxes. Across from her, Kianna stood on a wide stool, an apron swallowing her tiny form, and was bagging cookies and chattering faster than a scolding squirrel.

His heart clenched at the sight. Was this what he'd missed—what they'd missed—when he and Silvia parted ways? He rubbed at the ache in his chest.

Chapter Six

For the next two days, Silvia fought to wipe away the memory of the look on Pierce's face when he'd seen her interacting with Kianna. He'd stared at her with such open longing that the days when they'd been a couple had slammed into her. When they'd been headed for more than dating. When their lives had been so intertwined, nothing could separate them.

Until he turned his back on her. He'd said he wouldn't leave the ranch to travel like she wanted to do after college. He'd pulled away from their relationship. At least it felt that way.

In those few moments at the restaurant, all his desire for them to be together and have a family shone in his expression. Kids on the ranch. A house close to his parents. Her giving up her dreams and buying in to his. But that wasn't what happened. She hadn't been able to stay in Ashville.

So what about now? Her father wanted her to take over the restaurant. If she did that, her life of traveling would be over. No way could she run a business in Ashville from halfway around the world. How would that even work?

Why did the men in her life always consider her dreams fluff and their wants something solid? Was she not allowed to plan a life outside rural Arizona?

She pulled up to the cookhouse at the Bar X Ranch, Macie Calloway's place, and climbed out to deliver their lunches.

Bruiser, Macie's little beagle, raced up to her. She bent down to stroke the silky ears as Bruiser jumped up to lick her face.

"Bruiser, leave her alone." Macie patted her leg, and the dog ignored her.

"I see training is going well." Silvia grinned as Macie snorted a laugh.

"A well is a hole in the ground that I may have threatened Bruiser with yesterday." Macie's threat lost all credence when she scooped him up and kissed him on the head. "Remind me why I rescued a puppy instead of an adult dog, already trained and perfectly obedient."

Silvia laughed. "I don't think the shelter has many of those perfect dogs. Besides, Bruiser is the sweetest dog I've met in a long while."

"What you need is to go to that shelter and get a dog for your dad. Pete's always had a dog." Macie set Bruiser down to let him run circles around their legs. "I think his stroke happened because he was so sad about losing Dandy."

Dandy had been her father's yellow Lab. That dog followed him everywhere, even had a spot in the restaurant office where he slept while her dad worked. Dandy went on the runs to deliver lunches and was probably more popular than Silvia had ever been. The dog was the sweetest thing and lived longer than most dogs. She'd missed Dandy more than any human when she left Ashville.

Except Pierce.

"I'd better get these lunches delivered." She opened the hatch to lift out the wagon. "How's the Bar X doing?"

"Oh, you know. Good times. Bad times." Macie shrugged. She'd inherited the place when her husband died in a ranch accident two years ago. She'd had to learn the ranching business on the fly and had confided to Silvia how difficult it had been. Macie was the one friend from high school who liked

Silvia then and still liked her. They didn't get together often, but Silvia wanted to change that. Macie seemed to need a friend as much as Silvia did.

They chatted a while longer and exchanged numbers so they could text. It would be nice to reinvest herself in an old friendship.

Silvia hurried to deliver the lunches and get to the Forester Ranch. Talking with Macie had put her behind, but she'd catch up if nothing delayed her at her other stops. She had to handle the restaurant closing tonight since Jeanne liked Thursday night off to go to her Bible study group. It made for a long day, but Silvia didn't mind. The only downside was leaving her dad alone for so long, but so far they'd managed.

By the time she reached her last stop, she regretted exchanging numbers with Macie. What had she been thinking? The more friends she had here, the harder it would be to leave when her dad was back up to par. Everything weighed on her. Running the Chuckwagon. Befriending Macie. Pierce and Kianna, and the way they drew her to them. How did she cut ties when her heart cried out to settle in here? Did she want to cut those ties?

Then there was the vow she'd made to Keith and Steven after they died. To continue the adventures they'd planned. To carry on with their work. To be the wife Keith wanted her to be, even when his ideals stretched her out of her comfort zone. Yes, she loved the excitement of extreme sports. She loved new countries and new cultures. But maybe she didn't love them as much as she'd expected to. Or, maybe what she'd loved was sharing those experiences with Keith and Steven.

Now, the thought of continuing by herself was daunting. Where was the joy in conquering dangerous rapids or skiing a steep slope or hiking a little-known wilderness if she had no one to share that with other than nameless blog readers, or those who would buy the book? Had she loved the adventure more for the people with her?

She had to shake off these negative thoughts. Traveling had been her dream for so long, she didn't even remember when it started. As a young girl, she'd loved reading about other countries, their cultures and unique places to visit. Seeing new sights and learning about different people was in her blood. No way would staying in Ashville make her happy. Not even if she had friends here.

Not even if Pierce was here.

After she dropped Kianna at the ranch that evening, she headed back to the Chuckwagon. The dinner crowd amped up the noise level in the restaurant. There seemed to be more people than usual on a Thursday night. Lonnie, their other cook, had trouble keeping up with orders, even with plenty of staff helping.

"What's with all the people tonight, Tilly?" Silvia had just finished ringing up a party of five and seeing them out the door. Tilly's braid had come loose and the circles around her eyes showed her exhaustion.

"They had a college fair at the high school this afternoon and evening. Families went to that and now want a fast meal before they go home." Tilly headed to the window where Lonnie called an order ready. Tilly pulled the plates down and looked at the ticket to check where the order went before hurrying off.

Silvia grabbed a pad and pencil, crossing to a table of newcomers to take their order. For the next hour, she ran from tables to the register, not a moment to rest. At least she didn't have time to dwell on memories of Pierce and his adorable daughter, which were fast becoming her go-to thoughts.

"Hey, kiddo, I've got to take this. It's Silvia." Pierce held up his buzzing phone as he opened the back door for Kianna.

They'd just returned from her first ride on a horse. The ride had been good for both of them. Quiet at first, Kianna soon became her talkative self, a sign of her recovery. She'd asked about a million questions about the birds, the deer they saw, the mountains and on and on.

As the door slapped shut, he accepted the call. "Hi, Silvia, what's up? Everything okay at the Chuckwagon?"

The creak of a chair came through. "We're swamped tonight. I've only got a few minutes, but I wanted to talk to you about Kianna."

His chest tightened. Was she saying she couldn't help him out anymore? He took a calming breath. "Is there a problem?"

"I don't know." She blew out a breath. "I may be off base here, but I think she's having trouble adjusting, or maybe there's something wrong at school. Did you notice her being quiet today?"

He frowned. "Yes, we went for a ride and she was subdued at first. I thought she was just uncertain because it was her first time on a horse." Had he been wrong?

"Look, I don't know for sure, but she was quieter when I picked her up today. Most of the time, she snaps out of it at the restaurant and loves helping me. Today was different."

"Different how?"

"She didn't bounce back to her usual self. It's almost like when you first arrived and she was so sad. I don't want to worry you, but maybe be aware that there could be something."

He scrambled for something to say as he went back over the past week and thought about Kianna's attitude.

"Hey, I've got to get back out there and help Tilly. I could be wrong, I'm certainly no expert." The chair squeaked again.

"No. Thanks for bringing this up. I appreciate your insights." Pierce clicked off and stared out across the pastures. He'd have to talk to his mom about this, too.

After the evening meal, Pierce sent his mom to pick out something for Kianna to watch before bed. Tomorrow they could talk about school. Kianna was more open in the mornings. He loaded the dishwasher and cleaned up from dinner, just finishing when his mom came back into the kitchen.

"She's all settled. Do you want some tea or coffee?" His mom flicked the switch to warm up water in the kettle.

"I'll have some decaf." Pierce grabbed a pod and stuck it in the coffeemaker. When the drinks were ready, he carried them to the table and sat across from his mom. It was good to have her up and around again, after the past two days of bed rest.

"What's the news from Mr. Norton? Was he helpful at all?"

"First, he says Chet doesn't have a leg to stand on. His offer to you is unrealistic, and he needed to have stats and more information to be believable."

"Well, your father used to make deals on a handshake."

"Those were with people who offered fair deals. Chet Mason is trying to cheat you out of what is rightfully yours." Pierce sipped his coffee, wondering how his mom would react to his thoughts.

"Mom, are you okay with me taking over running the ranch? I was gone for years when I should have been here. Quinn's in California with Ashlyn and I still don't know about Caleb. I'm sorry we all deserted you." He swallowed hard at the thought of his parents facing the hardships of ranching on their own.

"Do you intend to stay long-term or is this a passing fancy?" His mom's question cut deep. She had every right to ask. He had to be straight with her, and with himself, too. Was he ready for this? To settle down here and do the hard work to make this ranch successful?

What about Silvia? Just seeing her again brought back all those dreams they'd had together. Except their dreams never meshed.

And now? Did he want to explore his feelings for Silvia? Did she feel anything for him anymore? He didn't know all that much about her life since high school, but he knew she'd been married.

No matter what, his life now meant pouring himself into the land that had been in his family for generations. He didn't want this heritage to be lost. Even if he never married, maybe one of his siblings would have a child interested in taking over the ranch. Maybe Kianna would want that.

"Mom, I am here for good. I'd like to build up the herd again. To bring the ranch back to what it was or maybe figure out some other ways to make it profitable. I'd like to get Quinn, Caleb and Ashlyn back here to see what they think. I haven't seen them for years. Why don't we see if they will all come for a visit? A reunion of sorts. We can hash out plans for the ranch with them."

"I don't know. Your sister and Quinn have her television show in LA. I'm not sure they'd want to leave the spotlight to come here. It depends on their filming schedule."

"And Caleb?"

His mom gripped her teacup with her twisted hands and lifted it to her mouth. She took a slow sip, her gaze riveted on the table. Finally, she set down the cup and sighed. "Caleb is…struggling. He's had some things happen and needed time away."

"What does that mean?" Pierce remembered his youngest brother as a jokester, always trying to make people smile. Pulling pranks that were funny but often got him in trouble. He'd been the class clown throughout school.

"While you were out of touch with us…" His mom pressed

her hands against her eyes. When she looked at him, tears glittered but didn't fall. "You were overseas when it happened. A little over a year ago, Caleb and some friends were goofing around. They thought it would be great fun to hop a train. Something they'd never done."

"There aren't any trains here. Why would they do that?" Pierce swirled the dregs of his coffee in his cup. His mom's tone told him this wasn't a story with a happy ending. What had his brother done this time? All his pranks were harmless. How had this been different?

"There was a new boy who'd moved to town. This time, the prank wasn't Caleb's idea, but he didn't stop them. They all went to Holbrook and picked a place they thought the train would slow enough for them to jump on." She choked up. Pressed her fist to her mouth to hold back a sob.

Pierce rounded the table to the chair next to her and pulled his mom close. Her thin frame shuddered as she tried to rein in her emotion.

"You don't have to talk about this." He had to know the truth, but if the telling proved too hurtful, he'd wait to find out. Maybe he'd give Quinn a call. They hadn't spoken in a couple of years, but his brother would tell him the truth.

Why hadn't he kept in touch? The weight of his decision to shut himself off from his family pressed down on him. He'd wanted distance because the ranch meant too much to him. If they talked to him about the ranch or asked him to come home, he'd never have made it in the army. Not even after he made friends and felt at home there.

"It's okay." His mom pulled away. "Two of Caleb's best friends died that night. Caleb wasn't hurt physically, but he blames himself for what happened."

Pierce drew in a sharp breath. His baby brother had experienced such horror and he hadn't even known.

Chapter Seven

"Hey, boss, glad you could join us." Grady gave a salute to Pierce before signaling the other cowboys and cantering over to where Pierce sat on his horse.

Pierce had instated Grady as the official foreman only a few days ago, and he'd already gained confidence in his job. As for the new *boss*, Pierce almost wished he'd tied himself in the saddle. Sleep had been hard to come by the past few days. Everything weighed on him. His mom's news about his siblings, the state of the ranch's finances, Chet Mason's deadline, the cattle herd—everything needed attention, and he was only one person.

Plus, he'd talked with Kianna and she was struggling to fit in. So far, she hadn't found a friend. She'd always been shy with new people, and while she had regressed in her speech and actions after the trauma she suffered, she was catching back up under Silvia's and his mom's care, and of course his own. It might take time for her to adjust, because ranch and small-town folks were a different breed from big-city people.

Grady pulled his horse alongside Pierce's and leaned on the pommel to stare at the calves they'd rounded up. "Good-looking crop. They all seem pretty healthy. We have the vet coming tomorrow for shots. We'll have them ready for market in a couple of weeks and ship them out."

"How's the market right now? I haven't had the chance to check."

"Prices are up at the moment. It's a good time to sell. If we wait too long, there'll be a glut and you know what that does to prices." Grady turned down his thumb.

Pierce nodded. That had been the story ever since he was old enough to understand ranching and marketing. Some things never changed.

"What can I do to help? I need some work to counteract so many hours inside at a desk." Pierce shifted in the saddle. Even the work wouldn't blot out the problems he faced. What he needed was a concentrated time of prayer, but finding that time had become a battle.

"We're trying to get them all penned for tomorrow. We still have some strays in the brush up on that hill. You up for chasing them down here? I'll go up with you and give a hand." Grady nodded as Pierce reined his horse around and lifted his chin in acknowledgement. He signaled to the others where they were going. He whistled and one of the ranch dogs loped over to lead them up the hill into the trees.

"You getting a handle on things?" Grady asked.

Pierce snorted. "Hardly. Did you know how bad the books are? Dad used to be so meticulous. What happened?"

Grady patted his mare's neck and frowned at the ground before facing forward again. "Your dad was having issues with focus for a long time before his heart attack. He had Caleb take over the books, but then the accident happened. Caleb pretty much lost it. He wasn't keeping up, and by the time your dad realized what was happening, everything was the mess you're finding now. He tried to fix things…"

"If he had trouble with focus, there's no way he could have made sense of the mess I'm finding." Pierce reined his gelding over to a small stand of trees where the dog was barking. Three calves were huddled there, and he circled behind them to urge them down the hill to where one of the men would take over.

Grady found a couple more, and they continued to work their way up the hill. Pierce relaxed into the work, the rhythm and familiarity soothing him.

They were riding back down toward the ranch as the sun hit high in the sky. Pierce had removed his jacket to tie behind his saddle. He had plans to drive over to Pete Durham's this afternoon for a visit. If he grabbed a quick shower and ate his lunch on the way—and if he didn't talk to Pete too long—he'd be in time to pick Kianna up from school and take her for some ice cream. She would love that. He'd already messaged Silvia about the change in plans.

"Grady, thanks for handling the calves. I know you'll get them vaccinated and ready for transport. You know the drill, and that's a comfort. If you need any contact information, we'll look it up in the records. That work?"

The foreman nodded. "Last year, I helped because Caleb wasn't sure what to do. I should still have all the information in a file."

"Thanks. That frees me up for other matters."

"What are you doing about Mason and his offer? He'll be coming around with pen in hand, expecting your mom to sign. When's he due back?"

Pierce guided his gelding around a bush, holding him back when a rabbit jumped up and ran right under the horse's nose. "He'll be here later this week."

His stomach tightened at the thought. Sure, the man didn't have a claim to the ranch, but he still might get ugly at being denied what he wanted. If Pierce hadn't come home when he did, his mom would have already signed away the ranch.

And rightly so, since she wasn't in great health and all her kids had deserted her.

By the time they reached the ranch buildings, Silvia had already been by with the delivery. Pierce shoved down his disappointment. Lectured himself on having those thoughts about her. Why did she draw him so much? Their connection had happened years ago, and they had nothing in common anymore. He had other pressing concerns that needed his focus. He had no time for a relationship, and Silvia didn't want one, anyway.

He opened the door to the house and paused. Something was off. He stepped inside and listened. Usually his mother had music playing, a Christian radio station or some playlist she liked. The quiet was disconcerting. Even with Kianna gone, there was always some background sound.

"Mom?"

She didn't answer. He strode through the kitchen, where he'd usually find her making lunch. Not in the living room or den. He headed down the hallway to the bedrooms. "Mom."

A faint sound came from the bathroom attached to her bedroom. He hurried to the closed door and knocked. "Mom, you okay?"

"Pierce." Her voice wavered.

"I'm coming in." He gave her time to object, then opened the door. She was lying on the floor, her twisted hands curled into her midsection, knees drawn up. Her face was almost as white as the floor tiles.

"What happened?" He kneeled down, assessing if she had any injuries. Her pulse was rapid, a slight sheen of sweat on her forehead.

"I think it's just a flu bug or something." She moaned and drew her knees up tighter. "I've been sick a few times. I don't have the energy to get to bed." Tears glittered in her eyes and broke his heart.

"Come on. I'll get you to bed." He lifted her slight frame with ease. She weighed next to nothing. She still had her pajamas on from this morning. He'd rushed Kianna off to meet Silvia early today and left immediately to meet Grady and help with the calves. He hadn't thought to check on his mom. She'd always been so capable.

"What can I get you? Some crackers? Water?" He drew the covers up around her.

"I just need sleep." Her eyelids drifted down and then opened again. "Thank you. I was getting so cold."

"Maybe I need to take you to the doctor." He put his hand on her forehead, but she didn't feel hot. Her breathing had already deepened, and her color looked better. He tucked the blanket tight around her and left the room.

Another change of plans. No way would he go off and leave his mom when she was so sick.

"Hey, Silvia." Jeanne leaned around the office door. "Did you hear about Brenda Forester?"

Silvia glanced up from the order form she'd been filling out. She blinked, trying to switch gears from restaurant needs to community. "No, what about her? Is something wrong?"

"A couple of the cowboys from the Forester Ranch came to town and said Pierce found her semiconscious on the bathroom floor. She has the flu or something."

"Did he take her to the hospital? What did they find?"

"You know Brenda. She's like a mule being turned away from the barn at feeding time. Setting her heels in and not going where she needs to go. She refused to see the doctor."

Silvia glanced at the clock. Getting close to dinnertime. Pierce had picked up Kianna today, so she hadn't been to the ranch. "Why don't you make up a couple of specials and a kid's meal for the Foresters? I'm almost done here, and I'll take them out to Pierce before I go home."

Jeanne's eyebrows rose almost to her hairline. "I thought you were avoiding Pierce. How is taking him dinner avoiding him?"

"I'm not going because I want to see Pierce. I'm going to take dinner to Brenda, making sure she's okay. She always could make those boys do whatever she wanted. If she needs to go to the hospital or the doctor, I'll be able to tell and can push her to go." She drummed her fingers on the desk and waited for Jeanne to quit staring and get back to work—and hoped the intuitive woman hadn't noticed the warmth in her cheeks caused by the uptick in her pulse at the thought of seeing Pierce again.

She didn't know if Pierce had any skill in the kitchen. He'd been in the army. Probably every meal he ate he found at the chow hall or whatever they called it, or came out of a can in one of the premade meals.

When she knew him, Pierce hadn't been a good cook. He might be able to rope and tie a calf, mend a fence good as new, or get a piece of ranch equipment up and running with nothing but a little piece of baling wire, but when it came to domestic duties, he'd had trouble boiling water. Had that changed since they dated?

"Alright. I'll get those ready, along with the meals for you and your dad. I'll throw in some pie for dessert, too. That little girl is cute as a bug. Pierce sure is blessed to have her."

Jeanne clicked the door shut, and Silvia turned back to the order form. She had to submit this before she left for the day, but her concentration had flown out the window. Just the thought of visiting the Forester place again had sweat dampening her palms.

She opened a browser and clicked on *Brazil*, looking up the site for kite surfing. She and Keith planned to do this and include a chapter about it in their book. While not as challenging as most of the extreme sports they did, this one sounded like fun and something their readers might like to try. As she watched a video of the colorful kites billowing across the water, the zing she'd once felt at a new adventure didn't come.

After clicking to close the website, she buried her face in her hands. The little-boy scent of Steven wound through her memory. She missed his enthusiasm. His laughter. The feel of him as he snuggled next to her for a story. Her heart ached for her family. Ached like it might break in two.

The need to get back to work on the book washed over her. Every day, her connection to Steven lessened. Her son always loved the danger and excitement, from hiking up steep slopes to rafting through rapids. His laughter rang through remote areas that most kids never saw.

The emptiness in her arms nearly undid her. The memory of his wiggly body as she hugged him and he wanted to be off doing something brought tears to her eyes. As did the way he'd run off and then reverse and crash into her with a hug so tight she couldn't breathe. She hugged her arms around her middle and rocked in the chair, fighting the sobs that pushed for release.

A few minutes later, she pulled out of her misery long enough to finish filling out the order form and submit it. She shut down the computer, gathered her things and headed out the door to the kitchen to pick up the meals.

Jeanne gave her an odd look but was too busy with an early dinner party to take time to ask questions. Silvia breathed out a slow breath as she stepped outside with the two bags of dinners in hand. Getting grilled by Jeanne would have been the worst right now.

The sky was still light when she bumped down the Forester lane and stopped by the house. Kianna was playing with one of the ranch dogs, an Australian cattle dog by the looks of its spotted coat.

The back door swung open as she approached, and Pierce stood there, his eyes as dark as a deep forest tonight, his hair mussed and his close-cut beard scruffy instead of neat.

"You look like a horse that's been 'rode hard and put away wet.'" She tilted her head to study him as he cracked a slight smile over the old saying. At least she'd gotten a smile of sorts. "How's your mom?"

"She's resting. Hasn't been sick to her stomach in a couple of hours. Come on in." He held the door open, stepping to one side so she could pass. This close, she caught the scent of horse and outdoors, a freshness that drew her in.

"Go on into the kitchen. I'll be right there." He leaned back out the door. "Kianna, time to come in and wash up."

Silvia turned to watch him hold the door until his daughter dragged inside, her lower lip protruding in a pout.

"Hey." He picked up Kianna and hugged her. "You know you have homework and then we have to eat. Right?" Kianna's *homework* consisted of coloring pages that gave her something to do with all her energy.

"I know, Unca Purse." Kianna hugged him back and squirmed to get down, just like Steven used to do. Silvia's breath caught in her chest and spots danced in her vision.

Kianna raced through the kitchen, giving Silvia a quick hug before she disappeared down the hallway.

"You're probably here to see Mom, but I think she's asleep right now. I really don't want to wake her up." Pierce ran his hand through his messy hair and scratched at his cheek. "Is there something I can help with?"

She held up the bag. "I brought dinner for all of you. I

think Jeanne packed some soup and bread for your mom. If she can't eat it tonight, you can save it for tomorrow. There's a kids' meal with grilled cheese for Kianna and a meat loaf and mashed potatoes for you."

His shoulders hunched forward. "That's so nice of you. Tell Jeanne thank you from us. I'll put Mom's in the refrigerator and see if she's up to some later."

She handed over the bag. "Yours might need a little heating first."

"I don't mind." He grabbed the bag with one hand and pulled her in for a quick hug with the other. The move surprised her. She stiffened, then melted into him for just a moment.

It had been over a year since she'd had a hug like this, from a man who set her heart racing when he put his arm around her. Not since Keith died.

Dangerous. And yet, this was Pierce. From what she'd seen he hadn't changed that much. He still put his family—his people—first and went out of his way to see to their needs.

Pierce stepped back. She didn't want the moment to turn too awkward, so she swiveled to the counter and unbagged the food. Pierce stood there, arms hanging at his sides, looking a little lost. "How's it going with the ranch?"

He shrugged. "I'm learning the lay of the land. Slowly."

"Is Grady a help? I know he's young but he seems like a hard worker. He's certainly eager."

Pierce crossed his arms and leaned against the counter. "He is a hard worker. He lacks a little in experience, but makes up for it with enthusiasm. I'm just a little overwhelmed with everything."

Silvia folded up the bag, leaving it on the counter. "Give yourself time. You used to be the best when it came to running the ranch with your dad's help. I'm sure it will all come back."

Kianna raced back into the kitchen waving her coloring page for Silvia to admire. Silvia said her goodbyes and slipped outside while Pierce heated up their dinners.

Once outside, she paused to breathe deep. Seeing Pierce and Kianna in a family setting did something to her—scattered her thoughts and gave her longings she shouldn't be having. She headed for her car, forcing herself to focus on her dad and what they would do tonight to encourage his healing.

Chapter Eight

The Chuckwagon meat loaf, normally one of his favorite meals, held little flavor for him tonight. Pierce listened as Kianna chattered about training the ranch dogs, as if they needed training. He tried to express the expected interest. What had he been thinking, hugging Silvia?

Truth was, he hadn't been thinking. Hugging her had been as natural as slipping on his favorite shirt. She'd felt so right in his arms. Like she had when they were in high school.

Except they weren't. Weren't young anymore. Weren't under the delusion that life would be perfect and they had a happy ending ahead of them. Not anymore.

Now, they were two disillusioned adults who'd lived through some difficult times and had more tough issues to face. Silvia didn't want to be here. He did. The same story they faced in high school was being played out again now.

The same ending was inevitable. Wasn't it?

"Did you hear me?" Kianna was standing on her chair, leaning over the table to stare at him eye-to-eye. He'd tuned her out and missed an important response. He gave himself a mental shake to get back in the moment with his daughter.

"Tell me again. My mind wandered." He took another bite of meat loaf and potatoes, and waited.

"Yesterday, me and Silvia had to stop in the middle of the

road on the way here." Kianna shrugged as she settled back in her chair and picked up the second half of her grilled cheese.

"Why did you have to stop? Was something wrong?"

Kianna rolled her eyes, giving a very good impression of her mother exasperated with her dad. "You didn't listen to anything." Her dramatic sigh echoed in the dining room. "Elk. A million of them on the road. A million."

Pierce gave a low whistle. "That's a lot of elk. I didn't know we had that many around here."

"We do. We had to wait and wait while they crossed. Miss Silvy honked the horn and they all stopped and just stared at us." Kianna giggled. "I wanted to get out and chase them, but Miss Silvy said no."

"I'm glad. That could have been dangerous. What did Miss Silvia do?" Pierce took a sip of water, enjoying this story more than he thought he would. Trust Kianna to distract him from maudlin thoughts.

"She said we would be turtles." Kianna jumped off her chair and pantomimed the creeping vehicle. Pierce pressed his lips together to keep from laughing.

Kianna hopped back on her chair, picked up a french fry and dragged it through ketchup. "Those babies were so cute." Just like that, she was on to another story about school. Her mind was a mystery to him. She changed thoughts midstream and more than likely would circle back to the elk story, leaving him confused and scrambling to catch up.

By the time they finished eating, his mom was awake. While Kianna played in her room, he heated some soup and took it to Brenda.

"Silvia brought us dinner from the Chuckwagon." He carried a tray in and set it on the bedside table while he helped her sit up and put pillows behind her. "You don't have to be afraid I cooked."

A little color had come back to her face, but her eyes didn't have their normal sparkle. "I'm sure you know a thing or two about cooking now. Although it might only be how to cook a rabbit over a campfire, and I'll pass on that."

"Did I ever tell you about cooking a rat over a fire of dung? That was tasty." He laughed at the face she made. "I promise to avoid demonstrating my skills in that area. Besides, the dung here might not have the same flavor."

He pulled up a chair and held the soup bowl, uncertain whether to spoon-feed her or if she could hold the bowl and feed herself. She held out her hands, and they only had a slight tremor.

She took a few bites before resting the bowl in her lap as she studied him. "Chet will be back soon. I don't know that I will be up to talking with him. I guess we'll see how I feel in the morning."

"I can handle this, Mom. I wanted the chance to talk to Pete Durham, but haven't gotten over there."

"Why Pete?" She lifted the bowl and took another spoonful.

"Donald Norton suggested it. He said Dad used to confide in Pete before anyone else. He might have given him some insights that'll help with the ranch." Pierce took the bowl and handed his mom a napkin with a piece of buttered bread he'd warmed in the oven. Jeanne baked bread every day, and it was one of the foods he'd missed when he'd been overseas.

"Then go over there now." His mom nibbled a tiny bite of bread. "It's not that late. Pete should still be up."

"I can't go off and leave you and Kianna." What kind of son would he be if he left his sick mom with a rambunctious child?

"I'll be fine. I'm feeling better already. I'll sit here and watch a show until you get back. Take Kianna with you. She loves Silvia and it might do Pete some good to meet her."

"I just might do that."

After helping his mom and cleaning up the supper dishes, Pierce called for Kianna and slipped her jacket on her, and then they headed out to the truck.

"Where are we going?" Kianna climbed in her booster seat and buckled the seat belt.

"We're going to Miss Silvia's house to talk to her dad." He climbed in the driver's seat. The engine roared to life, and they bumped down the drive. He had to get the grader out and smooth this lane. Tomorrow. He sighed. How many times lately had he said that? Tomorrow was always full before it even arrived.

Lights were on at the Durham house. As Pierce parked, he mused that he missed Pete's old hound dog baying at him.

The door swung open as he and Kianna climbed the steps to the porch. Silvia was backlit in the entry, her hair caught up in a clip with strands hanging down her back. His breath stuttered in his chest.

"This is a surprise." She stepped back and gestured for them to come inside.

Kianna bounced forward and wrapped her arms around Silvia's thigh. "Hi, Miss Silvy. We came to visit your dad."

Silvia smiled down at her, but once again Pierce thought he saw that flash of sorrow in her eyes he'd glimpsed before. What had he missed in her life?

"Dad, you have visitors." Silvia led the way into the living room, where her father sat with a book. He set down the latest thriller by his favorite author.

"Pierce." He nodded toward the man, then focused on Kianna standing at Pierce's side, her caramel eyes wide as a startled deer's. "Who's this with you?"

"Pete." Pierce stepped over to shake her dad's hand. "This is my daughter, Kianna."

"You married?" Dad frowned. His gaze flicked toward Silvia, but he kept his focus on Pierce and Kianna. Her dad was always one to test if rumors were true.

"Kianna is my soon-to-be-adopted daughter. The daughter of my best friend." A shadow passed through Pierce's eyes.

He still carried the pain of that loss. Did he know about hers? About Keith and Steven and…? The thought of telling him soured in her stomach.

"Kianna, do you want to come to the other room and see my old playhouse?" Silvia held out her hand. "Pierce, can I bring you anything? Water? Coffee?"

"I'm fine, thank you." Pierce took the chair next to her dad's and nodded to Kianna. The little girl took Silvia's hand and went with her to her old bedroom that still had many of her toys from when she grew up here. When she'd returned home, she hadn't changed this room, but instead moved into the guest room. Her mom used to come in here and sit, and once in a while she caught her dad in here, his eyes moist as he reminisced about their early years.

"Oh." Kianna squealed at the sight of the wooden playhouse, complete with miniature furniture and dolls. She dropped to her knees and just stared for several moments. "Can I touch them?" Her eyes were full of wonder as she gazed up at Silvia.

"Of course. That's why I brought you in here. I used to play with this when I was a young girl. My dad made it for me."

"He made this house?" Kianna touched the painted wood with the scalloped trim. "Did he make these?" She reached in and picked up a small rocking chair.

"He made everything except the dolls. He made the beds and cabinets. A few of the things we bought." Every year, after she received the house, she'd opened some new furnishing on her birthday and on Christmas. In his spare time, her dad loved making little pieces to round out the playhouse.

"My mom made the comforters for the beds and the tiny doilies on the tables." Silvia reached past Kianna to pick up a metal pitcher and touch the doily that was so lacy and yet only an inch wide. Silvia had never learned to crochet. Didn't have the patience for it. But her mom had mastered the art, and they had this to remember her by.

She sat down beside Kianna, and they examined all the dolls. Kianna made up a game where they had a tea party. Silvia's heart warmed even more to the girl. Steven had been all about adventure and playing rough. He never would have played with this house. Too boring for him.

Kianna was so different. Yet, she had such charm and sweetness. She'd opened up since that first day Pierce brought her home. In such a short time, she seemed to have adjusted to a different lifestyle and to the loss of her parents.

"What have we here?" Pierce came in and kneeled by Kianna. His scent—pine and outdoors—filled the room. He'd smelled the same years ago, and she hadn't forgotten.

"Unca Purse, look at this." Kianna held up the intricately carved rocking chair. She put it down and settled a tiny teddy bear on the seat and started them rocking. Silvia had done the same the Christmas she received both the chair and the bear. She remembered the wonder of it.

"That's pretty amazing." Pierce traced the scalloped eaves as he looked at Silvia. "Did Pete make this for you?" His eyes were a deep moss-green in this light.

"He did. He and my mom." A lump tightened her throat. "They spent years adding to it."

"I'm impressed. This thing belongs in a museum or some-thing. It's a work of art."

She turned to look at the house with a new perspective. He was right. The house was a treasure, collecting dust here in her old room. Maybe she should look into donating it. She'd heard about a museum of miniature houses in Tucson. Maybe they would like to put it on display.

"Did you get what you needed from Dad? He doesn't re-member everything but is doing pretty good." She placed the doll she'd been holding back in the living room of the house.

"I wasn't sure he'd be able to talk, but he had no problem. He's recovering better than most of those I've known who had a stroke."

"His was a lighter one. He still struggles with walking and doing physical activities like cooking. I don't know how soon he'll be back at the restaurant." She wanted to push him to get well, but she also wanted to prolong this time with him. She'd missed a lot with her parents and treasured this time. Getting back to work might be her focus, but that meant less time with her dad. Who knew how long he had left?

"How is your mom?" She dragged her thoughts from her worries and looked up at Pierce.

"She's better. She ate some of the soup you sent and a little of the bread." Pierce's smile reached his eyes as he studied her. "Thank you again for that. And for our meals."

"You make the bestest grilled cheese." Kianna peeled back the comforter on a bed, put a doll in and covered her up.

"Thank you." Silvia smiled. "I didn't make them, I just delivered the goods."

Pierce sank down to sit on the floor next to her. Kianna continued to play. Silvia needed to move away, but something held her in place. She'd never been able to distance herself from Pierce. Not without a lot of pain and heartache.

"I talked to your dad about some problems with the ranch.

Chet Mason is insisting Mom agreed to sell to him, but the contract he wants her to sign is bogus. The ranch is in trouble, and your dad shed some light on why." Pierce's low rumble lulled her into leaning closer to him.

"What's going on?" The quaver in her voice spoke volumes about how he affected her. *Move away.* She straightened and leaned on her other arm to put some distance between them.

"Turns out my dad invested in some quality livestock. He wanted to improve the herd. I remember him talking to me about this, but those cows are almost all gone. Your dad thinks they ended up on Mason's land and he kept them. He thinks Dad tried to get them back, but didn't want to go to the law with such a serious accusation. He didn't have proof."

"Wow, that is serious." Silvia read the trepidation in Pierce's forest-green eyes.

"It is a serious charge, and not one I'm ready to make." Pierce rubbed his hand down his face, the scratch of his whiskers loud in the quiet.

"What are you going to do? Does anyone else know about this?"

"I don't know. If it's true, it's possible he sold those cows, but if he did, the brand would have shown as Forester Ranch, the *FR*, not his stylized *CM*."

Silvia squeezed his hand. She hadn't meant to touch him, but the forlorn look in his eyes captivated her. She'd always been a sucker for the underdog and a sucker for Pierce Forester.

His green gaze swung to her, and the air stilled in the room. Her thoughts stuttered. His focus dropped to her mouth.

Silvia surged to her feet. "If you'll excuse me, I have to get Dad ready for bed. He can't stay up too late or he won't sleep." She rushed from the room before she babbled any more nonsense.

Chapter Nine

Kianna was quiet on the trip home. Pierce needed to get her to bed, or she'd be cranky all day tomorrow. She'd sure loved that dollhouse. Maybe he should think about building her one for Christmas. Would Pete want to help? He'd made that one for Silvia, so he had the knowledge, but did he have the dexterity? Something to consider.

The night air was brisk when he stepped out on the porch after getting Kianna settled. His mom was asleep again, her color much better. He shrugged on his jacket and settled in on the swing, coffee in hand. No way to sleep right now. Not with the memory of Silvia's touch.

Movement to his left caught his attention. Grady materialized out of the gloom. "I thought I saw you come outside. Wanted to report on the calves."

"Want some coffee?" Pierce lifted his mug. "Or we can go inside, where it's warmer."

"Out here is fine." The swing creaked as Grady settled beside him. "And I have my own." He lifted a travel mug and took a sip. "Besides, who'd want to miss this display?" He motioned to the black canopy overhead and the plethora of twinkling stars. The Milky Way was bright, looking like someone spilled glitter across the heavens.

"Vet get all the calves inoculated?" Pierce settled back, enjoying the view.

"Yep. All done. They're all counted and ready for pickup. I've arranged everything for them to be taken to auction. Prices are still up, so that's good for us."

"That it is. Thank you for taking that on."

They were silent for a few minutes. Pierce debated talking to Grady about his concerns, since Grady had been here all along working with his dad. Maybe he knew something about the missing cows. And as the acting foreman…

"I talked with Pete Durham tonight." Pierce paused as Grady turned to look at him. Then he went through all Pete had said. Grady nodded along as if this wasn't news at all. Something tightened inside Pierce. If Grady knew about the cattle and the discrepancy in the books, why hadn't he said something?

He finished, and they were silent again. A shooting star arced across the sky in a downward slope before winking out. As children, Pierce and his siblings would make a wish if they saw one. Those childish games didn't hold appeal anymore, but he needed something to help with this dilemma.

Lord, here I am again. In a mess. At least this time I'm not getting shot at and my men aren't in danger. But, please. Give me wisdom. That might be a bigger request than keeping my team safe in action.

He finished his coffee, the liquid almost cool. Grady shifted on the seat next to him. Crossed his ankle over his knee.

"Your dad." Grady cleared his throat. "He had trouble with Mason. The cows disappeared, but he didn't confide any suspicions to me. I had my own, and they all pointed to Mason. The man is as slippery as a fresh-caught trout. There have been rumors about him stealing cattle, but nothing proved. Not sure there's anything you can do about it at this point."

"When did Dad buy those cows? I'm having trouble finding anything on the books and following the trail. It looks like he bought them a couple of years ago, but then there's nothing."

"Yeah, that sounds about right. I think we had them at least a year when they disappeared. We have about fifty head left. A couple of the heifers gave birth this past spring. I kept those calves separate for the auction. They'll go for a higher price. If they'd been heifers, we'd have kept them." Grady rubbed his hand up and down his leg. His jaw muscles bunched.

They talked a bit longer before Grady wished him a goodnight and headed for his cabin. Pierce shook off his regrets. Looking back didn't help. He was here now and had to look at how to move forward.

His fingers were aching from the cold. He'd come out without gloves. He set his mug on the swing seat beside him and stuffed his hands in his pockets. The peaceful night settled around him, easing his worries. Closing his eyes, he spent some time in prayer, something he should have done before now. If he needed answers, God had them. He had to trust.

He opened his eyes again. Saw a second shooting star. Thought of Silvia.

There'd been a connection there tonight. They still had something between them, just like in high school. Something about her called to him. But she had her own plans. He knew she only intended to stay in town as long as her dad needed her. She hadn't changed for him years ago, and she wouldn't now. He had to put her aside.

If only she wasn't around almost every day.

A thump sounded from inside the house. A small cry. He grabbed his mug and leaped up from the swing, sending it swaying wildly. The door slammed closed behind him as he set his mug on the entry table and rushed down the hall to the bedrooms.

A soft sob came from Kianna's room. He cracked open the door. She was lying on the floor, curled in a ball. He hurried over and picked her up. She snuggled into him and his heart did a slow roll. He'd loved this child while his friends were still alive, and he loved her more now. He'd do anything to ensure her future and give her the home she deserved.

"I want my mommy." Kianna's whimper tore at him. She hadn't asked for Keisha often, but each time hurt. He had no way to give her the one thing she wanted most.

He pulled her close and murmured in her ear. She relaxed and fell back to sleep. He tucked her in and stepped softly out of the room.

Was he destined to fail at being her dad and caring for the family ranch? To fail at everything he tried?

We need to talk, Silvia.

Her dad's words echoed in her head as she prepared the box lunches Monday morning. The last thing she wanted to do was talk. Not after Pierce brought up all those memories the other night. He'd almost kissed her. She'd almost let him.

She yanked off a piece of tape to fasten a sandwich wrapper and reached for the next one. The one good thing to happen today was that the restaurant was busy with hunters up here to scout their areas. Jeanne had been so rushed she hadn't had time to question Silvia's foul mood. Poking the bear, so to speak, was Jeanne's specialty.

"Is this the last of them?" Chance Baker, a recent hire and new to the area, paused beside her.

"Those boxes are ready. I'm just finishing this up. Then I'll clean the counters and be out of your way." She nodded at Chance.

"I'll put them in your car for you. I've got a few minutes."

He lifted the boxes to the trolley and wheeled them to the back door.

She wiped down the counter as Chance came back in and carried out the last of the boxes. Silvia called goodbye to Jeanne, grabbed her purse and headed out the door.

Her phone buzzed as she slid in the driver's seat and closed the door. She fastened her seat belt as she accepted the call. "Hi, Pierce."

"Silvia." He cleared his throat. "Is this a good time to talk?"

"I'm getting ready to head out with my lunch deliveries but I can spare a few minutes. What's up?" Silvia settled back against the seat, trying not to consider how this would set her back timing wise.

"I wanted to thank you again for playing with Kianna while I talked with your dad."

Silvia laughed. "She's an amazing child. I enjoyed watching her play."

"I also wanted to mention before you pick her up today… I've been giving what you said some thought. She's been crying for her mother the last few nights." He paused, clearing his throat again.

"Pierce, I'm so sorry."

"I don't know what to do—how to help her through this. What do you say to a child who's had her whole world torn apart?" He sniffed and she was reminded of his tender heart. Of course, he'd want to solve Kianna's hurt and sorrow.

"I know it's an old adage, time healing wounds, but you do have to give her time. The stability you're providing will go a long way to helping her heal. She's already come a long way since you arrived in Ashville, right?"

"That's true." He sighed. "How do you always know the right thing to say?"

"In truth, I don't. I just say what makes sense to me." She closed her eyes against the burn as she recalled those first weeks and months after her family died.

"Well, you helped set my mind at ease. Thanks, Silvia. I'll let you get to your deliveries."

She said goodbye and hung up, taking a few moments to settle before she started her car. Talking to Pierce felt so natural, but also dangerous. She had to leave Ashville soon.

By the time she was on the way to the Forester Ranch, she'd run through every scenario possible to figure out how to leave Ashville early. Her phone rang, and she connected through the car. Her agent.

"Hello."

"Silvia, dear. How are you doing? How is your dad?" Marissa Leachman always sounded like she'd had the best day ever. So bright and vivacious. Never said an unkind word, even when she reprimanded a writer on a missed deadline.

"He's getting better, but it's slow. His speech is pretty good, but small motor skills have a ways to go." Silvia steered into a pull-off area, more like a wide spot in the road. Cell service was spotty here in the mountains, so it was better to stop than have the call dropped. Marissa had been trying to reach her for several days, and they'd been playing phone tag.

"That is good to hear. Any timeline yet on when you'll have the rest of the book to me? The publisher is asking."

"I have to get those last three adventures in so I can write about them." The same thing twisted in Silvia's stomach as always when she thought about going without Keith and Steven. She had to get past that. They were gone, and nothing would bring them back.

"Well the analytics show your scheduled posts are doing a good job retaining your audience. I used that to convince the publisher to give you more time.

Silvia swallowed hard. "I'm almost at the end of the scheduled posts."

Marissa softened her tone. "Your readers love your authenticity. Why don't you share some of what happen…"

"No." Silvia pressed her hand to her mouth. She wouldn't share her tragedy.

"Okay, let's talk about your book. Have you thought about using some of your earlier trips to include in the book and fill it out instead of waiting to try something new? I know you and Keith planned some you haven't done yet, but you have plenty you could draw from." Marissa's soothing tone took the sting out of hearing Keith's name aloud.

"Those probably wouldn't have the same impact. They weren't as extreme." She frowned out at the field stretching east from her car. Cattle dotted the pastureland, and in the distance a herd of antelope grazed and rested in the tall grass.

She'd never considered the easier trips they'd taken while building up to the more extreme treks. Their readers were those who wanted to do extreme sports, or those who wanted to read about them. Maybe Marissa made some sense. Not everyone was ready for the danger of a top-scale rapids, or hang gliding, where the air currents were so dangerous they could rip a glider to shreds. Or paragliding, which should have been safe…

Her breath seized. Black spots danced across her vision. She closed her eyes, fighting the memory of Keith and Steven plummeting to the ground.

"Silvia. Silvia. You still there?" Marissa's voice sounded tinny and distant.

"Yes, I'm here." She swallowed hard, focusing on the idyllic scene in front of her, not on the horrific one in her mind. "I'll consider that. Right now, I've got to finish my deliveries."

"Okay. I'll call in a few days and see what you've decided.

I think this might be a good way to go." The kindness in Marissa's tone made her eyes sting. She signed off and dropped her forehead to the steering wheel, fighting to get her emotions under control. To shove the pain back into a corner so she didn't have to feel anything.

Grady greeted her as she stepped from her SUV. "I was hoping nothing was wrong. You're a little later than usual for a Kianna day." She always dropped the Forester lunches early on the days she was bringing Kianna to school. Grady followed her to the back and lifted out the wagon.

"I had a phone call and pulled off to talk. You know, calls and the mountains."

"Don't we all. Sometimes feels like we're on another planet from all those city folks." Grady grinned at her, his blue eyes sparkling.

Kianna came racing from the house just as Silvia lifted the wagon back into her SUV, her backpack bouncing on her back. Pierce followed his daughter. "Thanks for taking her to school." He looked like he wanted to say more but she was running late and they both knew it.

Pierce headed back to the house as she climbed in her car and started the engine. A truck roared down the drive and slammed to a halt near the house, gravel spraying up behind the tires. Chet Mason stepped out and strode toward the back door.

"That man is angry." Kianna's small voice wavered.

Silvia turned and took the child's hand in hers. "Don't you worry. Your dad and grandma will be okay." That was when she saw the lunches on the seat for Pierce and his mom.

Chapter Ten

The sound of the truck engine combined with the spitting of gravel set Pierce's teeth on edge. Chet Mason had arrived with all his superiority intact. The next few minutes promised to be far from pleasant. His mom was asleep again, and Kianna was on the way to school. He didn't want either of them involved in this scene.

He grabbed the paperwork and stepped out the back door before Mason reached the steps. The big rancher halted when he saw Pierce, his beady eyes narrowing to slits.

"Where is your mother? My business is with her." The man could intimidate a grizzly bear, or thought he could. Pierce stood his ground.

"She's not feeling well. You'll deal with me or with no one."

"Did she sign the papers? We had an agreement." Mason held out his hand, and not for a shake.

"I advised her against signing this. I'm listed as the co-owner of this ranch. You and I did not shake on this deal." Pierce took the papers in both hands and slowly ripped them in two. "Besides, your deal with my mom cheated her out of what was rightfully hers. I've never seen anything this underhanded."

"She didn't tell me you're co-owner." Mason's face reddened. "My agreement is with her, and I want to talk to her. Let your mom tell me the deal is off."

"My mom is sick." Pierce leaned forward. "You enjoy intimidating sick women? Is that it?" Pushing too far wasn't advisable, but Pierce's pent-up emotions boiled to the surface. He had no grounds to accuse the man of stealing cattle. Yet. But he had the proof right here that he'd tried to get this ranch well below value.

"I offered a fair price." Mason's jaw jutted forward. His fists clenched at his waist.

"Fair? Fair for who?" Pierce's laugh was hollow. "You offered less than half the market value for the land and for the cattle. You didn't even address the value of the grazing rights, which, as you know, go with the ranch."

"Prices are falling. What I offered is fair." Mason eased back, his gaze drifting to the side as he spoke. The man didn't even know how to lie effectively.

"You are no longer welcome on this ranch." Pierce drew himself up and took a step forward. "Anyone who tries this with an elderly woman who has health issues isn't much of a person. Leave now and I'll let this go. Bother my mom again, and we'll get the law involved."

Mason's face turned bright red. For a moment, Pierce thought he would throw a punch. Instead, the man backed up a step. "This is not the end. You'll leave again. When you do, your mom will sell to me. And my price won't be as generous then." He turned and strode back to his truck.

The accusation about the cattle hung on the end of Pierce's tongue. He wanted to fling those words after the man. It took all his will to hold back without further proof.

The engine roared to life. Chet backed around, his tires digging grooves in the yard as he left. Pierce watched him bounce down the rutted lane, glad for once that he hadn't gotten around to grading it smooth.

"I thought for a minute I'd have to step in and help you throw him off the ranch." Grady stepped up beside him. Pierce hadn't even noticed him walking over. And, oh, good, Silvia stood beside Grady. She'd seen him at his finest today.

He fought the residual need to punch something and nodded at her. "Silvia."

She lifted a couple of boxes and held them out to him. "I brought something for you and your mom. I'm hoping she's better today." She glanced down the lane, following the spiral of dust on the road as Mason drove away.

"She is better. Thank you." He had to remember his manners. "Do you want to come in and see her if she's awake? I know she'd love the company, even if it's only for a few minutes."

"I'm heading back to lunch and to get the boys lined out for this afternoon. I'll be by later to catch up." Grady slapped him on the shoulder and strode away.

Pierce focused on Silvia. Despite his still roiling emotions, he appreciated how she looked. Dark jeans with black boots that came up to her knees, and a bright blue top of some silky material that waved and flattened against her in the breeze. A flowery scarf around her hair, the ends hanging down her back, completed the outfit. She was gorgeous. More beautiful than she'd been in high school.

"I really don't have time. Kianna's waiting in the car. After I drop her off, I have one more delivery to make." She grabbed one of the scarf ends and twisted it around her finger.

"I'll walk you back to your car. I'm sure Kianna was upset when Chet showed up."

"She was, but I assured her you'd handle him." Silvia shot him a smile that felt like an arrow to the heart.

He paused, turning to face her. Opened his mouth to speak, closed it, then spoke. "Silvia, where did we go wrong? What happened to us back then? I was so sure…" He jerked his gaze from the stricken look in her eyes. Had he overstepped? The question had been dogging him for days.

Silvia chewed on her bottom lip before brushing a strand of hair back from her face. "Maybe we were just too young. We didn't know how to handle our different ideals. You wanted the ranch and home while I wanted travel and adventure." She shrugged. "We both needed to mature."

He shoved his hands in his pockets. "You're probably right." And she was, but he also wanted to know if she'd missed him as much as he missed her? Did she ever think of him? Long for the connection they once had?

They continued on to the car, walking side by side. The back of her hand brushed his, catapulting him back to all the times he'd wrap her smaller hand in his. When they'd been so close, they finished each other's sentences.

A lifetime ago.

"I've got to go." Silvia hesitated as he finished reassuring Kianna and closed the rear door. "I know what we had once was good—better than good, but that's long past. Now, you need to focus on the ranch and your responsibilities here."

"You're right. It's a mess."

"Have you thought about calling your brothers and sister? Maybe they need to give you some input. Or they need to be here to see your mom." She shrugged. "I'm not trying to tell you what to do, but I know they care."

"If they cared, they'd be here." Pierce clamped his teeth together as hurt flared in her eyes. "I'm sorry. I don't have a number for Caleb. I did call Ashlyn and Quinn, but they're too busy filming to get involved with the ranch. Their words, not mine."

* * *

His sad gaze said he hadn't meant to be so harsh. Pierce had to be hurting. Not only had he left home when he was supposed to be there to help his father, but he'd also stayed away for fourteen years. What brought him back? Just his father's death, or was there something else? Did it have to do with Kianna? She still didn't have the entire story there.

She guided her SUV home after a long day at the restaurant, having dropped Kianna with Brenda earlier, her thoughts filled with the man she shouldn't be thinking about. The man who consumed her thoughts way too much.

Pierce was a protector. That was why he grew up wanting to stay on the ranch and protect the land inherited by his father and grandfather. She'd bet that was why he went into the military and into Special Forces—to protect those he cared about. Maybe that was why he returned. To protect Kianna and his mom.

There was something so appealing about a man who shielded those he loved with such fierceness. He gave up everything to see to them.

She turned into the driveway and raised her eyebrows at the sight of her father sitting outside on one of the porch chairs. They didn't live in town, but not as far out as the Foresters. Their place was quiet and on a nice day like this it was peaceful in a way living in town never would be.

After switching off the car, she grabbed their dinner from the back, along with her purse and some paperwork she needed to look over, and headed for the porch. "Good day to sit out here." She leaned down to drop a kiss on her dad's stubbly cheek. His hazel eyes were clear today. He'd lost some of the paunch he'd gained in the last few years. Maybe he'd go for a walk to their pond with her. She debated if the ground was smooth enough for him to traverse.

"Have a seat." He nodded at the other chair. "It's good to relax after a hard day."

She set down her things and sank into the chair. "How do you know it was a hard day?"

He chuckled. "Aren't they all?"

She laughed with him. "I guess most are. We have that in common. We tend to hit it hard from sunup to bedtime."

They sat in silence, watching a herd of deer come over the rise to drink at the pond, grazing along the way. Silvia never ceased to marvel at the grace of the animals. A few of the young ones were playful but never strayed far from the herd.

"We need to talk." Her dad's gaze settled on her, the reason he'd been sitting out here waiting for her. Her stomach clenched, and she picked at a loose thread at the hem of her top.

"What about?"

"The restaurant." He lifted his left hand to scratch at his salt-and-pepper hair, leaving strands sticking up. "Silvia, it's time for you to settle down. You're good with the people here. Good with the restaurant. It's time for you to take over and run things without me."

"No." The word came out sharper than she intended. "You need to be there. Even if you can't do deliveries, you should be at the restaurant. Those people love you and miss seeing you."

"And what am I going to do?" A hint of red flared on his cheeks. "I can't even make coffee by myself. If I tried to help, I'd make a mess of it."

"Then come sit and talk with people. You sit around here all day, anyway. Start by coming with me in the morning. I can drop you back home when I do the deliveries. If all goes well, you can stay longer as you gain strength." She leaned forward. How could she make him see how he needed the restaurant as much as the people there needed him? She wasn't the one they gravitated toward. It had always been her dad.

"I can do that, but we both know I'll never run things like I did before." Sorrow dug grooves at the sides of his mouth. The Chuckwagon had been his life...well, along with her mother. Losing both of them might start him on a slippery slope to worse health. She'd seen it happen before, to people who had been married as long as her parents had.

He pushed against the chair arms and lifted to his feet, swaying a few seconds before gaining his balance. "Silvia, I haven't asked you for much. But I'm asking you now to stay here and run the Chuckwagon. This is your mom's and my legacy, and we did it for you."

He shuffled to the door and went inside. She sat frozen in the chair. That had been a low blow. He knew how much she loved to travel and do extreme sports, even though she had some doubts about continuing. Those doubts were temporary. Her blog followers expected extreme adventures from her, not the daily grind of running a restaurant. If she stayed here, she'd lose every bit of ground she'd gained over the years. Maybe even the book deal.

Maybe even herself.

They were both quiet through the evening, picking at their dinner, and her dad retired early. She waited until he'd had time to get to sleep, then fixed a hot tea and slipped out to the porch to look at the stars. If she stared at the sky, she could pretend to be elsewhere. Pretend to have her life back. Have Steven back.

Her throat tightened, and her eyes stung. Would missing him ever get easier? Sure, she missed Keith. But she and Keith had been together because of the adventure, similar goals and, yes, a kind of love, just not a great romance like her parents had.

Would giving up all her dreams be the end of her? Of who she was? How did one find contentment in a place that was the opposite of what they wanted? Her goal had been to come home, get her dad well enough to take over the restaurant again, then continue on with her adventures, start posting to her blog and sharing extras on her newsletter, finish writing her book.

Now what? Because doing that on her own held less appeal every day.

The rumble of an engine preceded the lights bouncing around a curve in the road. Someone headed the back way to town a little late. Not much would be open at this hour.

The lights turned into her drive, and soon the truck came to a stop by her SUV. Pierce climbed out and headed to the porch, his long strides eating up the distance.

He stopped at the bottom of the steps, his hands in his pockets, shoulders bowed. "I came to apologize. I didn't mean to snap at you earlier." He turned to stare off toward the pond, although it was too dark to see anything.

"Come sit down. Want some coffee or tea?"

He climbed the steps and sank into the chair her father had used earlier. "No thanks. I can't stay long. I put Kianna to bed, but sometimes she has bad dreams. I never know when she'll cry for her mom."

He cleared his throat and continued, "Her mom and dad were my best friends. I was babysitting Kianna when they died in a car accident. They named me her legal guardian but…" He dropped his face into his hands, and her heart ached for him. She almost reached out to him.

Almost.

"I couldn't reach Caleb, but I called Quinn and Ashlyn again. Asked them to come home. They both said it would be best to sell the ranch and put Mom in a home somewhere."

His breath hitched. "Neither of them seem to care that doing so will be a death knell for Mom. Her life is that ranch. All her memories of Dad. Of us."

Silvia leaned forward and placed her hand on his arm, the corded muscles tight. "Then figure a way to keep the ranch. Do what you need to do for your mom, for Kianna and for you. What is right for you?"

He stared up at the stars before meeting her gaze. "I want to make the ranch successful again. I'd like to provide a home for Kianna, and for my mom."

"So what's stopping you?"

"Right now, the ranch is barely making ends meet. I may have to let a couple of the hands go and they've all been here for years. That's not an easy decision."

"Don't give up yet, Pierce. There's got to be a way to make it profitable. You mentioned the books are a mess. Maybe you'll find a way to stabilize the ranch income as you straighten out the finances."

He leaned forward, elbows on his knees, head bowed. "I don't want to disappoint my dad more than I already have."

She sucked in a breath. He'd always carried responsibility like a heavy load. "I don't think there's any way you could disappoint your dad…or your mom. They loved you so much, your mom still does."

He turned his head to give her a small smile. "You're right. I need to remember that." He sat up, slapping his palms on his thighs. "Well, I'd better get back home. Thanks for the talk." He hesitated a moment. "I wish you'd consider staying in Ashville"

She sat back as he strode toward his truck. And there it was. Their different paths keeping them apart.

Chapter Eleven

Silvia settled in a church pew toward the back of the sanctuary and took a sip of her latte. She had the day off with nothing much to do after church. Driving three hours to Flagstaff to shop didn't interest her, and she needed nothing. Shopping just for fun had never been her happy place.

She should have slept in instead of coming to the early service. But she'd been awake by five, as had her dad. She'd convinced him to go with her to church—a first—and seeing him talking with longtime friends had been worth the rush to get them ready and here before nine. Maybe he'd even go to lunch with her afterward.

Even better, maybe he'd go to lunch with his friends. If he had fun, he might be willing to spend some of his day at the Chuckwagon. Being part of that life he'd loved for so long could only help speed his recovery.

Did she even dare hope he might one day return to run the restaurant? It had been a tense week since he'd insisted she take over running the Chuckwagon permanently, and she didn't know what to expect. Had he grown tired of the work? Had he lost heart when her mom died? The Chuckwagon had been their dream, and no one cooked like her mom. Although Jeanne came close.

Her dad made his way over and settled next to her in the pew. He smiled at her. Smiled. Almost symmetrical, too.

Something inside her relaxed for the first time since convincing him to attend church.

He lifted his hand in a wave, and she turned to see Pierce and his mom across the room. She smiled and nodded at them. They hadn't talked again since the night he came to the house, except in passing when she dropped off Kianna. She'd thought about asking him what he'd done about the ranch with all the problems, but she didn't have the right. If he wanted to talk, he'd come to her—or to her dad. He seemed to value her dad's opinion.

Pierce's dad used to stop by the restaurant or the house almost every day. He'd often disappear into the office with Pete and they'd talk over matters that concerned them. Losing such a close friend might also have contributed to her dad's reluctance to work at recovery.

The service was good, and she shifted in the seat as the pastor reminded them of the necessity of consulting God before they made decisions. She hadn't consulted God in a while. The last time she'd cried out to Him had been on a lonely hillside as a paraglider plummeted toward the earth.

Where had He been then?

She shut out the rest of the service, thinking about the book she needed to finish and what to do about her dad and the restaurant. Maybe this afternoon she'd follow Marissa's advice. Take the time to go back through their older blog posts to see if any of those would work to fill out the book. Her limbs felt weighted at the thought of abandoning the plans she and Keith had made. He would never agree to this—the book was supposed to be all-new material with a specific focus on extreme sports. Not recycled material. The picture of disappointment mirrored in Keith's and Steven's eyes brought tears. She blinked them away as the congregation stood for the final song.

"Ms. Silvy." Kianna raced toward her, braids flying, beaming a smile as big as a mountain. "Ms. Silvy, guess what?" The girl bounced in place, clapping her hands.

Silvia kneeled down and had to grin. "Okay, let me guess. Must be something fantastic." She tapped her finger against her lip as Pierce walked up behind Kianna. "I know. There are piles of presents under your Christmas tree."

Kianna's mouth rounded in an *O*. "It's not close to Christmas." She put her small hands on her waist and shook her head. "We're going to watch some fires today. Enormous fires. In the forest."

Silvia glanced toward the mountains. She hadn't heard about any fires, but they were always a concern. A fire could wipe out thousands of acres of forestland and wreak havoc on the natural habitat of the wildlife here. And why would Pierce take his daughter close to one?

"That's not quite accurate." Pierce's low rumble drew her attention from the hills. He cupped the back of Kianna's head. "We're going to a fire tower, where they watch for fires. Remember, Kianna? If they see them, the fires can be put out early and not cause so much damage."

"Oh, yeah." Kianna nodded. "The fire tower is tall, and I get to climb to the top. We can see a long way from there."

"That sounds very exciting. Maybe you'll see some deer or elk on your way there." Silvia stood and stuffed her hands in her pockets to keep from hugging the little girl. How she missed small arms wrapping around her and sloppy kisses on her cheek.

Kianna leaned closer. "I want to see a bear. We talked about bears at school. There's one bear who smokes, and that's not a good thing, but he's a good bear and helps put out fires."

Pierce coughed and covered a grin with his hand. "Is that Smokey Bear?"

"Yes, do you know him?" Kianna swung around to look up. "He's really big and wears a funny hat."

Silvia chuckled. Nothing like a child's perspective to see things in a different light. "I believe his name is Smokey. That doesn't mean he smokes. That would be a bad thing, especially when you're fighting fires."

Pierce's chest rose and fell. "Silvia's right. Smokey is a good firefighter."

"Oh." Kianna's little forehead furrowed, and she nodded. Then she brightened and bounced in front of Silvia again. "Ms. Silvy, can you come with us? If you're scared, I'll hold your hand while we climb the tall tower."

Laughter bubbled up, threatening to spill over. Kianna didn't know how many dangerous things she'd tried. Climbing a fire tower would be simple in comparison.

"Ms. Silvia is probably working at the restaurant today." Pierce put a hand on Kianna's shoulder. "Maybe we can arrange another time."

In that moment, she wanted nothing more than to go to the mountains with them. The book could wait. Her dad would be fine without her. Spending a day with Kianna and Pierce, stretching her muscles outdoors, gave her the first tingle of interest she'd had in over a year. Even if it was only a rough mountain road and a climb up a fire tower. Listening to Kianna's take on the wildlife and the scenery would be more fun than anything else she'd done in a long time.

"I don't have to work today. I'll have to take my dad home and change clothes, but if you have room, I'd love to go."

Pierce's eyebrows rose. Kianna danced around their feet. The moment stretched out. Had she overstepped? Maybe Pierce didn't want her along. Maybe he wanted this time for just him and his daughter.

"I have to take my mom home, too, and we need to change.

Church clothes aren't the best for tramping through the woods." They both looked down at Kianna's wide eyes, her hands clasped together under her chin, and Pierce added, "Why don't I call in a picnic order at the Chuckwagon? We'll pick you up in half an hour and then stop by to pick up the lunch on our way to the mountain."

Her pulse thrummed at the idea. A picnic. A day away. Not that it was a day with Pierce, but a day of fun with a child that reminded her of Steven. That was all this was.

"Stay here. I'll be right back." Pierce jumped from the truck and went into the Chuckwagon to grab their lunch. He'd gotten them changed and ready to go in record time, thanks to Kianna's enthusiasm. His mom reminded him to take a blanket to sit on and some jackets in case it turned cold. Fall in the mountains meant the weather could turn in a minute. Sunny and warm and then cloudy and chilly. He needed to be prepared.

Silvia looked perfect when he picked her up. She wore short hiking boots, jeans and a long-sleeved Henley in a dusky blue. She'd braided her hair. It hung over one shoulder almost to her waist. The mix of golds and browns set off her mocha eyes to perfection.

She was so beautiful his heart ached. Did she want to catch up with him, learn more about his past as much as he wanted to know hers? He'd known about her blog but hadn't read the posts past the first few. Seeing her happy with another man proved too painful. Much too painful.

He strode back out and put the bag in the well behind the driver's seat. He had Kianna's booster seat in the middle behind him, so both he and Silvia could see her and talk to her. She'd already been chattering away to Silvia, telling her everything about school and the ranch and her grandmother being sick. Silvia might need earplugs before the day was over.

"Everyone ready?" He handed a small bag to Silvia. "I thought we might need a snack on the trip up. It will take at least ninety minutes to reach the fire tower."

"Which one are we going to?" Silvia settled back as he pulled out and headed toward the highway. "I remember there being two of them we used to talk about, but I've forgotten their names."

"I debated between PS Lookout and the one that overlooks Wildcat Point. We'll go to the one near Wildcat Point. I can't recall the name, but it's usually manned at this time of year. If we have time, we can go both places." Pierce picked up speed on the highway and they left Ashville behind. Pasture-land gave way to scrub trees and piñon pines.

"Look what I have here." Silvia opened the smaller bag and peered into it.

Kianna leaned forward. "What is it?" She clapped her little hands, her eyes alight with interest.

"I think this is just for me." Silvia pulled a chocolate chip cookie from the bag. "Yum."

"Me." Kianna kicked her legs and held out her hands. "I want one. Please?"

Silvia laughed, the sound music in the cab of the truck. She looked back in the bag. "There are chocolate chip or peanut butter. Which do you want?"

"Chocolate chip." Kianna clapped her hands. "My favorite."

Silvia pulled out a napkin and wrapped it around the cookie. She handed it to Kianna before turning to Pierce. "What do you want?" She rolled her eyes. "As if I have to ask."

He grinned. "Peanut butter. It hasn't changed."

She wrapped a cookie for him and took a peanut butter for herself. No surprise there. They'd both loved peanut butter in high school. Back when neither of them had much money, they'd save their coins and split a peanut-butter cookie. If they were really flush, they'd share a peanut-butter shake. He hadn't had one of those since he and Silvia parted ways.

She broke off a bite of her cookie and popped it in her mouth. He kept his attention on the road but watched her from the corner of his eye. It would have been wiser to come up here without her, but when she said she had the day off, and Kianna looked at him with those doe eyes, he'd been a goner. Now, she sat in his truck, the scent of her soap or shampoo filling the cab with coconut and freshness.

"How long has it been since you've been up in the Black River area or up in the White Mountains at all?" He kept his tone casual. His mom said Silvia rarely came home, and he could hardly judge her. He hadn't been back more than a handful of times, either.

"When I was still in college, I came home a couple of times. I was so focused on getting my degree early and doing what I wanted to do that I took classes year-round as much as possible." She broke off another piece of cookie but held it in her hand. "Once Keith and I started our extreme adventures and sharing them online, I didn't come home at all. I never realized I could make a living doing it, but I could. We could. It just kept us on the move all the time. I still Skyped with my parents, but not as much as I should have. The few times I came back, I didn't go to the mountains."

Did she ever think about the memories they'd made here? He sure did. "I get that. I didn't come back much, either." A regret he had to live with. "Tell me about your adventures. What did you do?" He bit off a chunk of the now tasteless cookie. Did he really want to know what she and her husband had fun doing?

She turned to study him, and he kept his gaze straight ahead. No way would he show any of the emotions roiling around inside him. She didn't need to be burdened with his regrets.

"If there was a challenge out there, Keith and I tried it. From hang gliding to snowboarding out of a plane to rafting class V rapids, we did it. I've been to more countries than I have to states in the USA."

"I don't even know you could snowboard out of a plane."

She chuckled. "Keith and I made good business partners. He was the ideas guy, researching extreme sports and the best destinations to try them in. And he was better with a camera. I was the one who did the most writing, and I took care of most of the marketing and social media to increase our audience."

Her tone held a hint of wistfulness when she talked about the travel, but was almost clinical about her late husband. Did she miss the lifestyle? Did she miss Keith?

"Why did you marry Keith?" He almost bit his tongue when the question slipped out.

She looked out the side window instead of at him. "We had similar goals. We both wanted to conquer the world, or at least its challenges. We both wanted to tell people what it's like to experience the highs of danger when they might not have the chance to do it themselves."

"You married for a common goal, not love?"

"I loved him, but our marriage was definitely more for convenience as we traveled and worked together. We didn't have that deep connection like my parents had."

Silvia glanced back at Kianna. Pierce hadn't realized how quiet his daughter had been. He looked in the mirror to see her slumped to the side, sound asleep, boneless as only a child or small animal could be.

"My one true love died a year ago." Silvia's words struck like an arrow to his chest. The air sucked out of the truck and he forgot to slow on a turn. The truck skidded sideways in the loose gravel. He lifted his foot from the gas pedal, then gave a little gas to pull out of the skid.

When he'd righted the truck and come out of the curve, he glanced over at Silvia. What had she meant? A lone tear trailed down her cheek, and she swiped it away. If she hadn't married Keith for love, had she later fallen in love with him?

"You probably know that Keith died in a paragliding accident." Her breath hitched, and she swallowed hard. "He loved taking chances. We both did. But that day wasn't a day like that. It was perfect weather, totally safe."

She smoothed her hand down her jeans, keeping her face turned away. He'd heard part of the story, but not all.

"What most people don't know is that it was our son's birthday. Keith took Steven up with him."

Pierce's hands ached from his grip on the steering wheel. She'd had a son?

"How old was Steven?" His throat was tight, his voice gravelly.

"Six that day. Almost the same age as Kianna. It was a tandem glider, and the operator cleared us to let Steven go up. It was his one birthday wish, to be like Mommy and Daddy." She put the back of her hand to her mouth, stifling a sob. "We triple-checked the rules. The operator said they'd flown kids even younger—if the wind was right and they were calm. But something happened, a change in the wind shear no one predicted, and the glider went down."

They were quiet until he made the turn toward the rugged road to the lookout. Wrapping his mind around the thought that she'd lost a husband and a son on the same day took all his concentration.

She cleared her throat. "What no one knows. Not even my dad." She swiped at tears again. "When they crashed, I ran to them, praying they'd still be alive. I fell. Rolled down the hill." Her sob filled the cab with so much pain he couldn't breathe.

"I was six months pregnant. My baby girl didn't survive that day, either."

Chapter Twelve

"Are we here?" Kianna rubbed at her eyes and leaned forward. "I don't see any tall tower to climb."

Pierce cleared his throat, hoping his voice didn't crack when he answered her. "We're getting ready to go up this steep hill. See it ahead?" He glanced back to see her nod. "It's going to be a little bumpy going up. You ready?"

"Yes." Kianna bounced in her seat, oblivious to the breaking hearts in the front seat of the truck.

He put the vehicle in gear and eased forward. Stretched his hand out and squeezed Silvia's arm. She had her head turned to the passenger side window, probably to hide her tears from his daughter. She'd carried this burden for a year. Hadn't talked to anyone. Lost her whole family in one day and still came back here to help her dad when he needed her.

She was as strong as any man on his Special Forces team. Maybe stronger.

He paused to put the truck in four-wheel drive when they reached the steep, rocky slope, keeping a close eye on Kianna. She might be scared of this ride. He'd seen grown people turn around and go back because the road was treacherous and rough.

"This is funner than Disney World." Kianna bounced and clapped. "Go faster."

Silvia blew her nose and turned to smile at him. "You're

raising an adventurer." They hit a big rut, almost cracking Silvia's head against the roof. She laughed aloud.

"No hands." Kianna raised her arms over her head like people did when riding a roller coaster. Pierce laughed along with Silvia, even as a pang for her loss reverberated through him. Her son had been the same age as Kianna.

Had this been what his mom meant when she mentioned Kianna bringing pain, but in a good way? Maybe being around his daughter would bring healing to Silvia. Not that she would ever forget her son or daughter or get over the loss, but perhaps that loss would be more bearable.

Now, he understood why she was only in town temporarily. Her need to continue the challenges she and Keith were doing. It must be a chance to recapture what she had with her husband and son. A chance to hold on to their memories even as they faded day by day.

Kianna's delighted laughs kept Silvia and him chuckling all the way to the top of the mountain. He turned the final corner and the lookout tower stood tall among the pines. Rocks dotted the landscape. A herd of deer jerked their heads up in the trees on the downslope, flicked their tails and ran away.

"The tower." Kianna leaned down to see to the top through the window. "That's far."

She was right. The steps wound back and forth up to the platform at the top. There was a small room up there where a US Forest Service person lived, or used to, watching every day to make sure there weren't fires starting anywhere.

"Let's go." Pierce opened the side door to catch Kianna as she leaped into his arms. She'd had her seat belt undone as soon as he shut off the engine.

Silvia met them at the front of the truck. She tilted her head back and breathed deeply. "I forgot how clean the air is up here. This is a perfect day."

Perfect. He wasn't sure he'd define it that way. Finding out the horror she lived through had been a huge setback for him. She'd had a year to adjust. He'd had minutes. His whole body still felt the impact of her revelation.

"Want to race to the top?" Kianna tugged on his hand. Her eyes danced with a challenge that reminded him so much of her dad, Dean. That man had always been up for something new. He met everything head-on—even dangerous missions.

"How about we all go up together, and you hold my hand?" Pierce grinned at his daughter's disappointed pout. "These steps might be big for you and I don't want you to fall. Your grandma would tan my hide if that happened."

Kianna stopped at the bottom of the stairs and studied him. "Tan your hide? What does that mean?"

Silvia leaned down and spoke in an exaggerated whisper. "That means she'd spank him."

Kianna gasped and clapped her hand to her mouth. She didn't smother the giggles that erupted. Pierce laughed along with her. "See, if you hold my hand, you'll spare me a spanking."

They climbed the tower, resting on the landings where the stairs turned, catching their breath and enjoying the view. They were disappointed to find the room locked, and the lookout gone. Pierce stood next to Silvia and pointed out different areas of interest that she might remember. He lifted Kianna up so she could see Ashville so far in the distance it made Silvia's miniature house look gigantic. Below them, a herd of deer came out of the forest and he showed them to Kianna before pointing out an eagle soaring overhead.

"Ready to head down? That picnic lunch is calling our names." Pierce took his daughter's hand and followed Silvia as she led the way.

At the bottom, they found a picnic table, and he pulled out

the food containers. Jeanne had packed sandwiches and chips, like Silvia did during the week. Kianna's was peanut butter and jelly with a side of carrot sticks and a bag of Cheetos, her favorite. Pierce and Silvia had ham sandwiches, which tasted better than they did at the ranch. Something about being out in the mountain air always made the food taste better.

"Can I explore, Unca Purse?" Kianna left her half-eaten sandwich and climbed from the bench. Her fingers were covered with cheesy orange crumbs.

"Let me wash those hands first. And you have to promise to stay close." He found a wet wipe in the bag and cleaned her hands and around her mouth. "Why don't you see if you can find some pretty rocks or some nice pine cones to take home? Here." He handed her an empty plastic bag, and she scampered off.

He and Silvia watched her explore as they finished their lunches. The pressure to acknowledge what Silvia had told him pressed against his ribs. "Silvia." He covered her hand with his. "I'm so sorry for what happened to your family. I didn't know. I can't even imagine how you managed."

She shrugged. Tears glittered in her eyes and she blinked rapidly. "You get by one day at a time. I spent several days in a hospital. I had them buried there instead of back here. Keith didn't have any family and my family didn't know him or Steven. They loved Switzerland, and I like to think they'd be happy with that resting place and being together."

She pulled a potato chip from the bag, broke off a tiny piece and dropped the bit to the ground, then broke off another. Strands of her hair had come loose from her braid, dancing in the light breeze. He fought the urge to smooth them back from her face.

"Is that why you want to go back?" He cleaned up his trash

and Kianna's. His daughter was under a huge pine, examining the cones that had fallen and adding some to her bag.

"I miss them so much." Her voice caught. "Part of me feels like I should build a little hut near their graves and just stay there with them. My babies."

The idea of ending her life of adventure and sitting beside their graves for the rest of her life wasn't good.

"And what does God have to say? What does He want you to do?"

Her mouth thinned to a narrow line. "God wasn't there that day. I don't think He cares about anything I do."

Silvia had trouble dragging herself from the truck by the time they reached her house. "Good night, Kianna." She leaned over the seat to see the little girl. Kianna had run all over the mountain area, and she loved it when they stopped and hiked part of Wildcat Creek. She'd been a ball of energy but looked drained right now. She hadn't even talked much in the last forty-five minutes.

Kianna waved. "Good night."

"Thanks for going with us, Silvia." Pierce's steady gaze and warm tone didn't have the usual effect of settling her. Not tonight. She had too much on her mind for that.

"Thanks for including me, Pierce. I've missed the mountains here." That part was true. She'd forgotten about the wild beauty and the hidden places she used to visit. The big meadows and the acres of trees stretching across the hills. Places that used to call to her before she left home.

The day had elements of fun, but what had she been thinking, opening up to Pierce like that? Telling him about Keith and Steven was one thing. Everyone in town had heard at least part of the story. But the baby? No one knew that part.

Now, Pierce knew. Because she'd always been able to talk

to him. Always confided everything to him. Trusted him with her secrets.

But that had been fourteen years ago. She had no idea how his life had played out. Had no idea what kind of man he'd become.

Well, maybe some idea. After all, he'd stepped up to take care of his best friend's daughter after that friend died. Not everyone would do that, even if they'd been listed as the child's guardian. And he cared for his mother and reached out to others for help on deciding what to do about the ranch. That took a strong character.

Maybe he hadn't changed so much.

Her soul felt battered. Physically, the day had been perfect. Being outdoors in the mountains. Getting in some climbing. The picnic lunch. Watching the wildlife.

But emotionally and spiritually, she'd taken some hits. Dredging up the past always hurt. She paused on the porch, her hand on the doorknob. Bringing up the past to Pierce had been different from any other time she'd had to talk about what happened. Yes, it hurt. But there'd also been some relief, maybe a bit of healing.

Spiritually? First, the pastor at church talking about listening to what God wants you to do, and then Pierce bringing up the same thing. Who was trying to get her attention? Them or God? Did He really care about her? If so, why hadn't He listened when she needed Him? Why hadn't He saved her family?

Why had He left her alone?

She rested her forehead against the wooden doorframe, her eyes stinging, her nose running. Every time she'd thought about this, there'd been a niggling in the back of her mind— a reminder that she hadn't stayed close to God. Hadn't listened to Him or consulted Him for a long time prior to her family dying.

If she'd stayed close, there weren't guarantees her family would be alive, but perhaps the accident would have driven her closer to God instead of away from Him. *God, I don't know what to do. Show me. I'm so sorry.*

Shuffling came from inside. She sniffed and swiped at her tears. She might need time alone right now, but she had responsibilities, the first one to her father. It was almost dinnertime, and he had to eat on a regular schedule.

She drew in a deep breath of cool evening air and then another. Pulled the door open and went inside. "I'm home. Let me put my stuff away and I'll get you something to eat." She injected as much cheer into her voice as possible.

The refrigerator held some leftover soup from the restaurant. She dumped it in a pan and turned on the burner. In the pantry, she found crackers and put them on a plate. She made them each a small salad and sliced an apple to share. Simple. Light. Healthy.

And she had no appetite at all.

By the time she had the table set, the soup was hot. "Dinner's ready, Dad."

He shuffled into the dining area and sat down without saying a word. Okay. Not a good day then. Had spending time with his friends been too much for him? Had she pushed too hard in getting him to go to church? The doctor said he should be fine going out for a few hours. Church hadn't been that long. Unless his friends kept him out too long.

She waited for him to pray, but the prayer was so short she hoped God didn't miss it. Her father stared down at his bowl and finally lifted the spoon.

"Did you have fun today? What did you do with your

friends?" She stirred her soup before picking up a cracker and breaking it in half.

He slurped the liquid from his spoon, and she winced. He'd never have done that when her mom was alive. Wouldn't have done it before he had the stroke either.

"Went to the Wagon." A trail of liquid spilled from his mouth. She leaned across the table to hand him a napkin.

"How long were you there?" She'd told his friend, Jeff, he shouldn't stay out for more than an hour or two. That he wasn't strong enough to stay out long. Why had she gone with Pierce? She'd ruined the whole day for her, for her dad, for Pierce.

He frowned. "Home by half past noon. Took a nap."

He set his spoon down, studying her. "What upset you?"

She shifted in her chair. "What do you mean?"

"I can tell you've been crying. Did Pierce do something?" His brows furrowed as he studied her.

What should she say? Pierce hadn't done anything, but if she didn't confess what happened, her father would make assumptions and confront Pierce the next time he came over. Maybe she could tell him part of what they talked about.

"I told Pierce about the day Keith and Steven…" Her throat tightened up and she had trouble swallowing. Would this ever get easier? Would the image in her head ever soften?

Her father stared at her as if waiting for more. He deserved more. He deserved the truth.

"I told you about the accident." She put her shaking hands in her lap and wound her fingers together. She should have told her dad everything. But she hadn't counted on him ever finding out. And the whole truth had been entirely too painful. She'd pushed the thought of her daughter into the back of her mind. Tried to forget. As if not having a baby to hold and nurture meant she'd never existed.

But she had existed. And every fiber in Silvia missed that tiny girl.

Her chest constricted until spots danced in her vision. Her dad blurred as she tried to suck in air. How could she tell him when she'd buried that sorrow so deep?

Maybe he didn't know. Maybe she wouldn't have to tell this story twice in one day.

Maybe she could go back in time and change what happened. A tiny sob escaped.

"Dad, Keith and Steven weren't the only ones to die that day."

Her dad pushed aside his bowl and leaned on the table. "What aren't you telling me?"

Chapter Thirteen

"Dad, I…" Silvia pressed her fingertips to her eyes. She wanted this day to end. Or start over with a different middle and ending. She'd tumbled off a cliff somewhere and was in a free fall, and didn't know where she'd land.

Nowhere good.

What to say to her dad? How did she make him understand her reluctance to talk about her little girl who died? The daughter she and Keith never had a chance to meet. The sister Steven didn't get to play with or tease.

The baby her arms still ached to hold.

Her whole body hurt. Not just her chest and throat from unshed tears. But everything about her. As if she'd landed from that free fall and crushed every bone in her body.

Was it possible to die from sorrow? Hadn't she asked herself that question over and over this past year? With no answer?

Oh, God, please. She had no more words. Didn't even know what to ask from Him. Something deep within her craved the peace He offered. Craved Him.

Calloused hands wrapped around her wrists and tugged. She kept her eyes closed but lowered her hands to the table, and her father wrapped them in a touch so gentle she felt it all the way to her soul.

"Talk to me, Silvia. Tell me what happened." His tone

didn't carry condemnation, just the love she always received from him. He might be disappointed in some of her choices. Might be hurt that she'd cut him and her mother out of her life. But he'd always loved her. There'd been no doubt.

So she told him. About the accident. About the fall. The baby she lost. By the time she finished, their soup was cold and her dad had tears trailing unchecked down his leathery cheeks.

"I'm so sorry, Silvia." He squeezed her hands before releasing her. "Why don't you go clean up and get comfortable? We can reheat the soup and talk while we eat. The hot water will help you the most right now."

He was always right. She nodded and rose from the chair. She wanted to say something but couldn't find any more words.

Later, her hair still damp and wearing her favorite yoga pants and an old T-shirt covered in dancing cats, she padded down the hall to the kitchen. She could hear the microwave running. *Please, don't let Dad have spilled soup all over getting the bowls to the microwave.* It might be selfish, but she didn't want a mess to clean up right now. Cleaning up the mess inside her had been hard enough for one day.

Pierce stood at the microwave, a spoon in his hand, while her dad sat at the table. She stared, open-mouthed.

The microwave dinged, and he pulled a bowl from inside and turned around. He smiled when he saw her. "Here's your supper all warmed up for you. Your dad just finished. Come eat."

Come eat. Such a simple directive that sent warmth through her. No one had done much nice just for her in so long. Keith had been more of a wait-on-me kind of guy and didn't seem to see her needs. Of course, Steven had been too young. By the time she came home, her dad hadn't been in any shape to do things for her, and she'd taken over the restaurant to run things. She looked out for others, not the other way around.

"Thank you." She settled in the chair she'd vacated earlier. Pierce pulled out the one beside her and sat down. Her dad's bowl was empty, with very little mess around it. Unusual, to say the least. "Dad, did you get enough to eat? I can heat some more for you." She glanced to her left. "Or for you, Pierce, if you're hungry."

"I think we're both good." Pierce touched her shoulder, the brief contact shivering through her. "I ate a sandwich on the way over and helped your dad heat his soup."

Had he cleaned up any leftover mess, too? She didn't want to ask in front of her dad and embarrass him. She nodded and lifted a spoonful of soup, suddenly ravenous. "What brought you over here?"

"I have a proposition for your dad. Something I need help with, and he has some expertise." Pierce leaned back in his chair, folding his hands together on the table.

"Something with the ranch?" She broke off a piece of cracker and popped it in her mouth.

"No. Although, he helped a lot with the information he gave me the other week." Pierce nodded at her father, who smiled. Exhaustion drooped his eyes, and she'd have to get him to bed soon. He'd had a long day with his friends and then with their emotional talk.

"So...with what?" She stirred her soup and took another bite, enjoying the mix of flavors in Jeanne's minestrone.

"I'd like to make a dollhouse for Kianna for Christmas. I have some materials and figure if I start now, I might get it done in time."

"Lot of work." Her dad's words were a tad slurred, a sure sign he was tired. "I still have my schematics somewhere."

Pierce sat up straighter. "That would be helpful. A big part of the job is figuring out the dimensions and fitting it all together. I've looked online at some plans, but none of them are as nice as the one you built for Silvia. Did you buy the plans?"

"Nope. Drew them up myself. Your dad came over and gave me some input. Helped a lot." The excitement in her dad's eyes was something she hadn't seen since she'd returned home to help him. Yet, she hesitated to cheer him on. His coordination was still off—by a lot. He had trouble with motor control in small things. What if he tried to help Pierce and became discouraged at his lack of ability? What if this caused a setback in his recovery?

But what if it didn't? What if helping with this dollhouse proved to be the thing that increased his skills? Even if he only advised, the enthusiasm he was showing had to help.

She finished her meal while Pierce and her dad planned and discussed possibilities. If even half their ideas came to fruition, Kianna would be one happy little girl come Christmas morning. Silvia's insides turned to a gooey mass as she saw how Pierce took on the role of being a dad to a little girl who wasn't his biological child. If he loved Kianna this much, how would he react to a wife and a biological child?

He'd be the best dad ever. Steady. Loving. Patient. If she remembered right, those were all traits his dad had displayed toward Pierce and his siblings when they were growing up. Traits her dad also showed to her.

And if she took the time to think back, Pierce had also been that way with her when they dated. So what happened? Why did he let her go in the end, refuse to support her interests and dreams of travel? Then turn around and leave home, anyway? As if he was okay leaving home, just not for her.

Which broke her heart—then and now.

* * *

Pete's eyelids were drooping, his speech slower and a little slurred. Pierce didn't want to end their talk but recognized the signs of exhaustion in the man. He put his hands flat on the table and pushed back. "I've taken enough of your time. I'd better get back home and get Kianna to bed."

"Is your mom doing okay?" Silvia had been so quiet he'd almost forgotten she'd been sitting next to him. Well, he hadn't forgotten exactly. Her presence shone a warmth on him that was hard to ignore. Being around her only intensified the connection between them. After the trip today, spending so much time with her, he shouldn't have wanted to see her tonight. Or that was what he'd told himself.

Truth was, he'd made up this excuse to talk to her dad about the dollhouse just to have a bit more time near her. Talking with Pete and planning with him had been fun. But the best part was sitting next to Silvia, even if they didn't touch or interact. Besides, he worried about her. After her story today and their rather intense conversation about God and faith, he needed to know she was alright.

That soulful look in her eyes told him she had some things to work through. Some issues to deal with. And he hoped she'd spend some time renewing her connection to her Savior. That was the most important. To her and to him.

When he'd left home, his faith had been on shaky ground. But being in Special Forces, putting his life on the line for others, had a way of making him see his need for that connection with God. Over the years, his faith grew, and he surrounded himself with a few soldiers like Dean, who were brothers in service and in faith.

He started as he realized he hadn't answered Silvia's question. "Yes, she's much better. She was watching a movie with

Kianna when I left. They should be done soon, and Kianna will be ready for bed. Mom, too."

"Good." Silvia gathered her dishes and took them to the sink. He stood and shook hands with Pete, promising to come back in a couple of days to help find those schematics for the dollhouse.

Silvia walked him out. They stopped on the porch and stared up at the night sky. There weren't as many stars tonight. Clouds had drifted in to cover much of the sky, the moon lighting their edges with a golden glow.

"Are you okay?" He had to ask. His arms ached to wrap around her shoulders. To let her head rest against his chest. How was it that the feel of her held close had never left him? Did she know all the times he'd been on a mission under a different desert sky and only the thought of her and their young love carried him through? Of course, then the guilt would come, because she had married Keith by then. And he wasn't one to love another man's wife. But he hadn't been able to erase the memory of her from his heart.

"I'm good. Feeling a little empty, I guess." She wrapped her arms around her middle and he noticed the chill.

"I hadn't told my dad about the baby. We talked tonight." Her breath stuttered.

"That must have been hard. Especially after our day and our talks."

Her lips pressed together, and she nodded without looking at him. Her chin wobbled. He had to do something. He put his arm around her shoulders and pulled her close. Her forehead thumped against his chest, and he tightened his hold. "I'm sorry you had to go through all of this. You've had quite the day."

She nodded. Stood there, not pulling back. But also not putting her arms around him. If she did, would he kiss her?

Like he'd wanted to do since the first day he'd returned and seen her at his ranch?

Like he'd wanted to do for years?

"I know you miss all the stuff you did with your husband, and you miss blogging about your adventures. What about doing some hikes around here and posting about those? We have beautiful country that's remote and interesting. I'd be willing to go with you on a few hikes or a fishing trip."

She tipped her head back to look up at him. Worried her lower lip, which made him suck in a breath. Gave a slow nod. "I can't go until next Sunday afternoon, but I could test the waters. See if my readers want to hear about something tame for a change. I'm almost out of material to write about trips I've done in the past."

"If my mom's arthritis isn't flaring up, I can ask her to take care of Kianna that afternoon. Unless you know a teenager who might like to babysit."

Her lips pursed in the most adorable way. "Let me check my schedule at the restaurant and get back to you. One of our servers, Tilly, is always looking for a little extra to help with expenses. She's the most responsible teen I've ever met."

"You mean nothing like we were?" He grinned as she rolled her eyes.

"Speak for yourself, Forester. I'm not the one who put that poor calf on top of the school building. Or the one who filled Mr. Matthews's desk with packing peanuts. Or the one…"

He covered her mouth with his hand, laughing as he did so. "Why do you think that was me? No one ever proved anything."

She snorted a laugh and pulled his hand away. "Because your partners in crime weren't as good at keeping their mouths shut as you were. It was all over the school, but I don't think any of the adults ever knew." She shook her head.

"Besides, I was your girlfriend. Everyone assumed I knew your every move."

"Okay, guilty as charged. But I wasn't alone."

She lowered her voice and leaned close. "But you were the mastermind. I know you were." Her eyes twinkled in the moonlight. The clouds scudding across the sky cast shadows over her features. Her coconut scent wove around him, twisting through him. He took a deep breath, forcing himself to focus on reality. Her dad was better every day. She planned to leave. He had to stay. Even if he lost the ranch.

Silvia stepped back. Her wary expression said she must have felt something she didn't want to feel. Or maybe he was projecting a vibe he hadn't intended to.

He took a step toward the edge of the porch, his arms empty at his sides. "Let me know about Tilly. I think that's a better option than having my mom watch Kianna for an extended length of time. I never know when her arthritis will flare up and she won't be able to do much."

"I will." She reached for the screen door and pulled it open. "Thanks for including Dad on your project. I haven't seen him this excited in a long time. I hope it all works out."

"Hey." He waited until he had her full attention. "I know he's struggling with motor skills. I helped him eat his dinner tonight while you were in the shower. I'll make sure he doesn't overextend. And I'll give him jobs he can do. I'm mainly interested in his experience and his direction."

"That, he can do." She wrinkled her nose in the cutest way. Just as she'd done in high school and stolen his heart. "I remember how bossy he can be. You might be tired of him before you even get started."

He laughed. "We'll see about that. Good night." He strode to his truck and drove into the night, his heart hammering. *Stolen his heart. Stolen his heart.* The phrase was on repeat, a mantra in his head.

That was years ago. Right? In the past. No way would he allow her to steal his heart again. He was older and wiser. She'd never stick around. Never.

Chapter Fourteen

Steam rose from the cup of coffee on his desk. Pierce tried to focus on the ledger pages he'd brought up, but his conversation with Silvia last night kept running through his head—as well as that thank-you-and-good-night-again text she sent. She worried about her dad. For good reason.

Pete had made remarkable progress since the stroke from what his mother told him, but he still had a long way to go. Silvia simply asked him to only use her dad for going over plans and not for the actual cutting and building. She worried that the frustration of not being able to do the work he once did with ease would be a setback. She might be right. Pierce didn't want to see Pete hurt if he fumbled.

He ran his hands down his face, the scratch of his stubble reminding him he hadn't taken the time to shave this morning. Should he let the scruff grow out and have a trimmed beard like he'd had right after he left the service? Women seemed to like that. Would Silvia?

His heart gave an extra thump. He liked the idea of her noticing. But he shouldn't. Why, oh, why, did he like her so much? Why wasn't there some local woman who loved kids and wanted to settle here in Ashville for life who attracted him? Why did he have to fall for the one woman who didn't return his feelings? Who would run away again at the first chance.

He dropped his hands, banging against the keyboard. The computer screen went crazy. The file manager popped up, and he noticed a separated drive he hadn't seen before. Why had his dad partitioned off part of his hard drive? Pierce clicked on it.

Two files showed up. Crane Cattle. And FSS.

Crane Cattle was pretty easy. He clicked open the file. He'd been searching everywhere for this information. This was the list of cattle his father had purchased when the Crane Ranch in Montana quit running livestock. They'd sold off their cattle, all of them top-of-the-line in their breed. All Red Angus. Not as popular as Black Angus, but they had similar characteristics. According to Grady, the reds were more docile, better mothers and tolerated the heat better than the blacks. That was why his father chose them.

He leaned forward to study the list and characteristics of the cattle. Each one had a pedigree and notes about temperament and health. In addition to the herd of Black Angus and Hereford cattle already on Forester Ranch, his father had purchased two hundred head of the Red Angus. Not that he would mix the breeds, but they could run together for grazing. Right now, they only had fifty head left of the reds, and one bull. What had happened to the rest?

He backed out of the file and clicked on the one labeled FSS. He jerked in the chair when the page unfolded with a list of Red Angus cattle. Did FSS stand for Forester Stolen Stock or was that just where his mind went because he'd been looking for them? His father had made a list of all the cows that were missing. He'd even made notes on the dates the cattle disappeared. If he did suspect Mason, he hadn't confronted him or gone to the authorities. Nothing had been proven. Mason had no cattle on his property that showed the *FR* brand. Why hadn't his dad pursued this?

These mountains were extensive, and they could hide cattle for a long time. If some hunter happened on them, they'd have no idea the cattle were stolen, so they wouldn't report them. The chances of his dad finding them or of Pierce doing so were almost nil.

He pulled up the books on the screen. His father had been friends with Walter Crane for years. He got a good deal on the cows and the bull, but still spent thousands of dollars to purchase and transport the cattle. The bull alone cost almost five thousand dollars, and that was with the good friend's discount.

Yes, they still had a few of the cows and the bull, but the bulk of the herd had gone missing. Just disappeared. How did a hundred and fifty cows vanish? The answer—they didn't. Someone drove those cattle off this land and took them some place.

At the time they vanished, all the cows had been in one of the farthest grazing areas of the ranch. They hadn't been taken up the mountain yet. The morning of the discovery, the fences were down. His father recovered about fifty head of cows, but the rest were just gone. From what Grady said, rain started that morning before sunrise. All tracks washed away, and mountain streams became impassable. His dad didn't even make notes about a search. Why?

A knock sounded on the outside door of the office. Pierce closed out the files and went back to the regular drive. He didn't want anyone to know what he'd found just yet. His dad kept this hidden for a reason.

He swung the door open and stared.

Caleb.

His youngest brother stood there, hands in his pockets, his dark hair sticking up at odd angles, whether by design or because he'd just dragged himself from bed, Pierce didn't know.

"Caleb." He stepped out and wrapped his arms around the

brother he hadn't seen in too many years. They were almost the same height, Caleb maybe an inch shorter, at six feet even. His always thin face appeared gaunt, his eyes sunken. "Looks like you ended up on the underside of the bull at the rodeo."

Caleb huffed a laugh. "Feels that way, too."

"Have you seen Mom?"

"No. Grady said you'd probably be in the office, so I came here first." Caleb's shoulders hunched forward even more at the mention of their mother. Something was off, but what?

"Come on in. Want some coffee?" Pierce pointed at the pot and the extra mugs he kept on hand in case Grady or one of the other cowboys came by.

"Thanks." Caleb poured a cup and then sank on to the sofa near the desk.

"What brings you home? I called you, but you didn't answer." Pierce took a sip of his coffee before getting up to toss it out the door and pour fresh. He sat again, the warm mug easing some of the chill that came from looking at Caleb. Something was seriously wrong.

"I've been..." His brother glanced out the window, his lips twisted in a grimace. "I've been going through a rough spell. I need to talk to Mom but it's not easy." He swallowed hard. Tapped his foot on the floor.

His eyes had that same look Pierce saw in Silvia's eyes sometimes. As if they'd seen too much or felt too much pain. And what did he even know about Caleb? That two of his friends died. That he'd disappeared. That he left rather than take on the responsibility of the ranch. Which Pierce understood.

"What's up?" He kept his tone even, not betraying his tumbling thoughts. He wanted Silvia here with him. Her steady calm always settled him. She seemed to know what to say, no matter the situation. And Caleb had always liked her.

"I—I need a place to stay." Caleb took another sip of coffee. Patted one of the fuzzy pillows their mom insisted on putting on the couch.

"This is your home. You know that. You're always welcome." Pierce leaned forward, hoping to encourage his brother to keep talking.

Caleb stared at the floor. "I need to talk to you, too, but it's hard. Can you give me some time? Seeing Mom will be bad enough."

Pierce noted again Caleb's sorrowful demeanor. He thought of Silvia waiting a year to tell anyone about her baby girl. He leaned forward and grasped his brother's arm. "I'm here whenever you're ready to talk."

"You heading to bed, Dad?" Silvia put the last of the dinner dishes in the drainer and shut off the water. She grabbed the sponge to swipe down the counters.

"I'll go in and watch a little TV first. From my bed." Her father's lips twitched a smile. For years, he'd been against having a television in the bedroom, but since the stroke, he enjoyed watching a show or two at night. And if he was too tired during the day, he'd lie in bed and drift off to something from the History Channel.

He paused in the doorway. "I thought Pierce would be over to talk about the dollhouse. Wonder if he changed his mind."

"I haven't seen him since Sunday evening. He hasn't been out at the cookhouse when I've delivered lunches this week, or at the house when I dropped off Kianna on Monday." That was odd, because he usually found a reason to come out and talk with her. This was Wednesday, and no one had said a word about him being away.

"I guess he'll show up when he's ready." Her dad shuffled down the hall to his room and shut the door.

She filled a travel mug with coffee, picked up her phone and a blanket, and headed for the front porch. Today had been beautiful with temperatures up in the seventies. The end of September was closing in and October promised to be much colder. She wanted to sit outside at night before the drop in temperature meant staying inside.

Once again, the night expanse of sky twinkled with stars, and the lack of cloud cover promised cooler weather tomorrow. She loved the night. The beauty of it. The similarity no matter where you were in the world. Well, at least being outside of large cities. The places she and Keith traveled to were almost always away from large populations, and the dark had always felt so comfortable. Almost like she was back home.

Her phone dinged with a text. Marissa. Again. Needing to know about the book.

Any book news?

I have six chapters polished.

Send them. Catherine wants to see.

I'll send them tomorrow.

She waited, but Marissa didn't write more. Six chapters were almost half the book. Maybe that would hold them at bay for a couple of weeks. Her amended deadline was fast approaching. She'd worked on doing a chapter on one of their early trips. It might work as a segue into the more dangerous ones. She might have time to polish that and send it tomorrow, just to test the waters.

A pack of coyotes took up a chorus not too far away. She closed her eyes and leaned back to listen. Barks alternated with yips, and then a howl that went up the musical scale. She used to read Steven a book about coyotes and always tried to imitate them. Steven usually howled with laughter, but he also tried to mimic her. The memory warmed her, instead of bringing the deep thrust of pain. *God, I miss him so much. So much.*

Her mother's heart might always miss her son, just as a part of her would always miss Keith. Their relationship had been easy, mostly. But Keith never made her heart pound, never drew her entire focus to him. She wasn't sure there was a way to explain the difference, but something in Pierce called to her on a deep level. And yet, their past would always stand in the way.

The coyotes faded off, probably chasing across the hills in search of dinner. Or maybe they had a midnight coyote get-together to attend. She smiled at the thought. That book of Steven's had a scene like that? Coyotes sitting around a campfire singing?

The sound of an engine took the place of animal songs. A truck turned in the driveway, headlights flashing across the house. Pierce. Butterflies skimmed through her stomach.

He parked at the edge of the yard and walked toward her with his effortless stride. She tried to picture him as a soldier, a fighter, and saw in that very grace the mountain lion inside the man. He'd have been good at what he did. Just as he'd been in high school, he now poured his all into the ranch.

"Evening, Pierce." She motioned to the chair beside hers. "Want some coffee? I think there's one cup left."

"I'm good. Thanks." He sank into the chair, an air of defeat, or dejection…something odd hanging over him.

"Dad's been wondering when you'll come by to talk about the dollhouse. Have you changed your mind?" She babbled words when all she wanted to do was wrap her arms around him and push away whatever was bothering him.

"No. I'll try to come tomorrow. Things have been a bit…" He paused so long she wondered if he'd gone to sleep. His head hung low, his expression shadowed. She wished she'd put on the porch light when she came out. But the light would have ruined her stargazing.

"A bit what?" She reached out and put her hand on his arm. Through his sleeve, the muscles corded taut under her touch. She pulled her hand back. Quick as a rattler, his hand darted out and caught hers, holding her fast. Her pulse did a slow roll and her breath caught.

"Caleb's home."

"What? Where's he been? Jeanne mentioned he took off, and no one knew where." The warmth of his palm against hers felt so right. She should tug her hand free but didn't have the heart. He seemed to need her.

"I don't know everything. He's…" His voice broke. Pierce drew in a ragged breath. "He's just out of jail."

"What?" Her exclamation released a cloud of white vapor. Coffee sloshed dangerously close to the rim of the mug. She steadied it with both hands, missing his touch.

Caleb had always been the jokster Forester sibling when at school but quiet at home. He enjoyed working on the ranch, but he also loved drawing and designing social media stuff. He used to hide in the barn to read books or took long walks by himself. She'd pictured him working in art or design, or maybe becoming a writer. Never had she pictured him arrested for anything.

Pierce huffed a laugh that held no humor. "Caleb's always been a bit withdrawn, but not at this level. He wanted me to give him a cabin to stay in, one that isn't used right now. He didn't want Mom to know he's here."

"What did you say?"

"I made him face Mom. He's staying in the house." A slight smile tilted his lips. Pierce had let his beard grow in the few days since she'd seen him. He'd trimmed it close, and the look worked on him. She gripped the cup tight to keep from touching him again.

"When Kianna came home, there was so much tension you could have roped it. But Kianna found out Caleb was her uncle, and he was a goner. She's been attached to him since then, and I think she is just what he needs." He rubbed at his temples and swiped at his eyes. Probably hoped she didn't notice.

"What can I do?" She settled the cooled coffee mug on the table next to her chair and clasped her hands together. Touching him right now would send a message she didn't want to give. They still had so much of their past that was hurtful, and they hadn't talked about it. Her life was uncertain, as was his.

But, oh, to be able to offer the comfort that he obviously needed. He lifted his head, his gaze intense, and she held her breath.

Chapter Fifteen

All thoughts of his brother fled as Pierce looked at Silvia and saw the longing in her eyes. The same expression he'd see when they were in class or at a public event and their only connection was an emotional one, not physical.

She's leaving. She's leaving. The voice that had been chanting in his head for days grew fainter. What if he convinced her to stay? Yes, things with the ranch were uncertain. If the ranch failed, he had little to offer her. Yes, he had a new daughter he was learning to raise. He had a mom who needed care. Now, a brother who also had needs he didn't understand.

But Silvia. He'd never stopped thinking about her. Never stopped aching to be near her.

Never stopped loving her.

"Why did you leave me behind, Silvia? I thought what we had was good. But you left like I meant nothing to you." He clamped his lips together. What had he been thinking, blurting that out? Laying himself bare. Leaving himself vulnerable to the one person with the ability to hurt him.

"Me?" She stared up at the night sky and toyed with the end of her braid. "I didn't leave you. You left me. I went to college. You're the one who joined the service and never looked back. I came home, and you were gone. You always said you'd never leave the ranch for me, so who did you leave for, Pierce? Because it wasn't me."

Her voice rose in volume. Not yelling, but more strident. And hurt. He heard it in her tone. Saw it in her eyes. In the rounding of her shoulders.

"I joined the service because of you. I thought if I proved I could travel away from here, you'd take me back."

"Then why didn't you tell me that?"

"Because you cut off all communication. I messaged you, emailed you, it all bounced back to me. You even changed your phone number." The frustration of those days rushed back and tinged his voice with gravel. Tremors skittered up his limbs. Had their separation all these years been a simple misunderstanding? A lack of communication?

"Someone stole my phone and every account on there got hacked. Email, social media, my phone number. It was all unusable. Why didn't you just ask my dad for my contact info?"

He scrubbed at his face with his hands. "Because I thought you blocked me. It was a pretty clear message. When I left, everyone was angry with me. I disappointed everyone in my life. No one took my calls. No one told me anything. It took years before your dad talked to me. Even now, I'm amazed he's willing to work with me at all."

"Oh, Pierce. I'm sorry. All these years I've been a little bitter toward you because I thought you didn't care about me anymore. Thought all those promises were a lie." The tears in her eyes glittered in the moonlight.

"I'm sorry, too. I was just trying to be what you wanted and made a mess of everything." He leaned forward with his elbows on his knees. "Can we put this behind us and be friends?" He wanted to ask about going back to the way they were, but that wouldn't happen. She'd need time to sort through all the past and the revelations they'd shared tonight. He needed time, too.

It was possible they'd never be more than friends. The

thought sent a pang through his chest. But he'd do whatever made Silvia happy. She deserved that. Plus, he had to think of Kianna now and what was best for her. And his mom. His brother. The ranch.

The list of responsibilities was endless. For just a moment, he missed being part of Special Forces. There, he understood the job. All he had to do was follow orders and watch out for his team. Except that didn't always work out well, either.

She brushed her hair behind her ear. "Yes, we can be friends. I'd like that."

"Thank you." He gave her hand a squeeze, wanting more but not willing to push. "I'd better get back home. Thanks for talking to me." He stood and stretched out the stiffness. "Are we still on for Sunday? Caleb can help Mom watch Kianna if Tilly can't. I still need to call her."

"I spoke to Tilly Monday night. She said she's happy to help with Kianna. She's expecting your call." Silvia unfolded from her chair with that extraordinary grace she always had. A cloud passed overhead, shadowing her features.

"I'll call her. Good night." He almost pulled her into a hug, but it would probably be awkward. Instead, he gave the end of her braid a light tug—something he used to do in the hallways at school. A signal to them both that he cared about her.

Did she remember?

A smile tilted her lips. She squeezed his arm—her signal back to him. Electricity tingled through him. Everything in him wanted to kiss her. Not tonight. Tonight, he'd leave her to mull over their conversation while he did the same. Maybe Sunday they'd be ready for more.

He climbed into the truck and watched as she picked up her coffee cup, tossed the cold liquid in the yard, waved and went inside. *God, is there a way for us? Did You bring us both back at the same time just to settle the past, or did You have other plans?*

His heart said, *please, please, let there be other plans. Plans that might include a future.*

He arrived home to find Caleb curled up with Kianna in her bed, reading her a book. Kianna's eyes rounded as Caleb used different voices or accents for the distinct characters. He didn't just read short kids' stories to her. Nope. He'd started *Stuart Little* after Pierce said *The Hobbit* might be too much. She loved the tale of the mouse and his adventures. Maybe a story about hobbits and trolls and dragons wasn't too much for her.

Not wanting to disturb them, he headed to the kitchen to get some water. He'd settle in the office for an hour or two to get some work done. He and Caleb needed to talk. Again. But right now, he just wanted to consider Silvia. Or to lose himself in work, if that was possible.

"You're back." His mom stood at the sink, a glass clutched between her gnarled fists. She set it on the counter and turned to him. "I'm heading to bed. Are you doing okay?"

"I'm fine."

"You know how I hate that word. Fine. It's a catch-all phrase and rarely means everything is good." She gave him that Mom look that stopped him in his tracks even today. "Where have you been?"

He shrugged. She didn't know he'd gone to see Silvia. *Like a moth to the flame* is what she'd say. "Just out for a while."

"You know, I may be old, but I'm not living in the Dark Ages. Pete texted me to say you were on the porch with Silvia."

"The information age strikes again." He chuckled. He hadn't considered his mom and Pete would text each other. Or care about him and Silvia meeting at night.

"Want to talk?" His mom had always cared. She'd been a sounding board when he didn't know what to do. Usually, she let him talk things out and didn't tell him what to do. She let him work it out on his own. But sometimes she had the best nugget of wisdom.

"Silvia and I talked. We sorted some things out from our past." He grabbed a glass from the cupboard and got some water.

"And?"

"I don't know. Right now, we agreed to just be friends."

His mom snorted, and that made him smile.

"Ready for a hike?" Pierce waited for Silvia beside her car outside the church. He hadn't offered to sit with her, giving her that time with her dad. She appreciated his thoughtfulness, but all during the service she'd been aware of him across the sanctuary, where he sat with his mom. Caleb hadn't been with them and she wondered about that. They used to all come as a family.

"I need to go by the house and drop Dad off. And change clothes." She shook out her skirt, not the appropriate attire for a hike in the mountains.

"How about I pick you up in half an hour?"

"Sounds good. I made up some sandwiches and snacks for us, and I dug out my old hiking gear." She opened the driver's door as her dad left his friends and made his slow way to the SUV. She wanted to rush over and help him, to make sure he didn't fall on the uneven ground. But he needed to do this on his own and not have her hovering while his friends watched.

"I'll bring a pack. I have some items for lunch, too. And waters." Pierce tugged a lock of her hair, his eyes warm as he looked at her. Since he'd visited the other night, she'd been pondering what he'd told her. She hadn't known her father refused to share her phone number. She'd been sure Pierce left her behind when he joined the service. He might have come home, but never when she'd been here. And he'd never contacted her. Everyone else in town had gotten her new contact info, and it never occurred to her that he didn't have it. His silence seemed like a sure message, and once she'd buried that hurt, she'd moved on with her life. Now, she wished she'd tried harder to connect with him and find out what he'd been thinking.

Yet if she had, she would have missed out on Steven. Her son meant everything to her. She'd never give up her time with him. He'd been so special.

She embraced the memories. Her son was gone. She had to learn to live again without dwelling on the negative every moment of the day. Keith and Steven both loved life to the fullest. They'd lived the way they wanted and died doing what they loved. Both of them would want her to go on living and to do what she believed was best.

Problem was, what did she believe was best? Going back out and following their game plan, or staying here and taking over the restaurant? Maybe she needed to make a list of pros and cons. But for now, she was determined to make today a positive experience.

Pierce tugged her hair again, and she met his gaze. "I think I lost you for a minute." His smile drew her in.

"You did." She reached out to squeeze his arm as her dad's passenger door slammed shut. "I'll see you in about half an hour."

"Sounds good." He headed for his mom and Kianna, who were just leaving the church. His long strides ate up the ground. She dragged her gaze from him and got in the car. The trip home was quiet as her dad leaned back in the seat and closed his eyes. He'd probably take a long nap, maybe two, today. He hadn't slept well last night, getting up to pace through the house more than once. Some nights were that way.

She'd just finished loading up her backpack when Pierce pulled up to the house. "'Bye, Dad." She waved at him from where he sat in his recliner in the living room. He waved back, and she pulled the door closed as she left.

"Where are we going?" A little thrill shot through her as Pierce opened her door and took her elbow as she climbed in the truck.

"I thought we'd go up to the West Fork of Black River. The campground is closed, but we can hike in and go along the river. I'd like to see how it's changed since the big fire."

"I remember reading about that fire." She snapped her seat belt and put her water bottle in the cup holder. "The devastation was horrible. Dad said it took years for the wildlife to come back. The herds are increasing, though."

"I've heard that, too. I'm hoping we see some deer or elk today. Did you bring your camera?"

"Yes. I even wrote on my blog that I'd be giving an update tonight about a hike today. This should give me some suitable material. I'll know then if my audience is interested in hearing about activities that are tamer than throwing yourself off a cliff or down a raging river."

They chatted on the way to Black River, the drive passing faster than Silvia remembered. They saw two deer, but it was the wrong time of day to see more. At the pullout near the river, they parked and donned their backpacks. Pierce offered to take some of the food from hers so her pack wouldn't be so heavy, but she waved him off.

The hillsides along the river were covered with trees, mostly conifers. Many had burned trunks with no life left. Butterflies flitted around ground-cover plants. The greens and golds from fall were evident in the low-growing ferns and other flora.

They hiked in silence for a couple of miles, listening to the water, the birds and the wind soughing in the trees. Even with the fire damage, the area was beautiful. She used her phone for some pictures, speaking into the notes app when she wanted to remember something.

Silvia had forgotten how much she loved these mountains. As teens, she and Pierce came up here with friends to hike and explore when they all had a rare Saturday off. They even had a swimming hole they enjoyed. Very few people knew about the place. Most of the river was too shallow for swimming, but there was one spot where it circled and the rocks were just right, giving the water enough depth for people to swim. Sort of. They'd at least get wet and splash around. She smiled at the memory.

Pierce paused up ahead, and she came up beside him. He nodded toward a grassy spot up the slope. "I don't know about you, but I'm ready for some lunch." His stomach growled, and he grinned.

She pressed the heel of her palm against her stomach to keep down an answering growl. "Sounds good to me." They set out the food on a light blanket she'd stuffed down in her backpack.

The chicken salad sandwiches she'd made hit the spot. Silvia swallowed, leaned back against a log and let her gaze travel over the surrounding slopes. "I love being in places like this. I'm reminded how insignificant I am. How alone I am, and yet not alone."

He took a long drink of his water. "I get that. What blows me away is being so insignificant and yet loved by God."

"I know." A glow settled deep inside her at the thought. She'd been reading her Bible and praying. A lot. God had given her so much peace about what she'd gone through. She'd never forget her loss, but was learning to live again.

"Hey, look." Pierce nodded across the river. Two deer were following a trail through the undergrowth, heading for the water. He and Silvia stayed quiet, watching. Three more deer stepped out of the trees and into sight. Pierce's hand covered hers and squeezed.

Silvia slipped her hand into her pack and eased out her camera. She put it on silent and took pictures as the deer drank and moved on. Their grace awed her.

One of them flung her head up, ears alert. The others froze in place. In a moment, they were bounding through the undergrowth into the trees, climbing the steep slope as if it was flat ground.

Silvia turned to Pierce. "What spooked them?"

He shrugged and gathered up their trash to put in a small bag, which he put in his pack. "I don't know."

He stood and held out his hand, helping her to her feet. She stumbled and fell against him. His muscular arm wrapped around her waist, holding her close. She looked up, and his intense gaze made her breath catch.

He lowered his head and brushed his lips across hers.

Chapter Sixteen

The next morning, Pierce leaned back in his office chair, staring up at the ceiling when he should untangle the mess in his father's books. But that kiss yesterday with Silvia had been on repeat in his thoughts all night long. Every time he tried to focus on numbers, the memory of her starry-eyed expression after they'd kissed made his breath hitch and his thoughts scatter like the stars in the night sky.

The kiss had been simple. Short.

He'd kissed other women. Not often, because he rarely dated, even when he'd been in the States on leave and had the opportunity. He'd kissed Silvia before when they dated in high school.

But yesterday… Yesterday was different. There'd been a connection he'd never felt before. Because they'd both matured? Were they ready for a relationship now, where they weren't when they were younger? Had it been more than misunderstandings that kept them apart?

Maybe it hadn't been God's timing for them to be together. Maybe they had lessons to learn. Life to live first.

His mind kept circling back to that moment. He'd felt it. From the look in her eyes, Silvia felt it, too. And hadn't been sure how to react.

They'd hiked another couple of miles before turning back. The sun was setting early, and he didn't want them still on the trail in the dark. The awkwardness after the kiss settled into a comfortable chat on the way home. They talked about Tilly watching Kianna at the house and discussed his mom's and her dad's health issues and their concerns for them. They talked about the ranch and how Chet Mason had actually backed off with the help of the documents Donald Norton had drawn up for him. They even talked about Quinn and Ashlyn, and what he could do to get them home for a visit and to talk about the ranch options.

That last thought dropped a lead weight in his gut. His father left the ranch to him on the condition that he provide a home for his mom. Not a problem. But Quinn and Ashlyn wanted him to sell the ranch. The twins had never been as invested in the family home as he and Caleb had, and they didn't want to hear about ranch woes from their oldest brother, the one they believed had turned his back on the ranch long ago.

He wasn't sure where Caleb stood right now. His brother had said little since coming home. He hadn't even explained why he'd been arrested and served time in jail other than it had been a misdemeanor. He'd spent time with Kianna and even helped Grady with chores and fence mending, but he kept quiet about where he'd been and what he'd done since leaving home.

Pierce sat up and focused again on the computer in front of him. Pete expected him to come by this evening and look at those plans for the dollhouse. He'd ask Caleb to go with him. If he and his brother worked together on this project, they might have some time to talk. He remembered more than once when his dad asked for his help when he was younger— not because he needed the help, but because working together might get Pierce to open up about his problems.

A sharp knock sounded on the outside door. Pierce turned. "Come in."

Caleb stuck his head in, hat in hand, hair windblown. With his dark hair and light eyes, he looked the most like Pierce. Everyone knew they were brothers. If they were closer in age, they might be mistaken for twins.

"What's up?" He beckoned Caleb to come in. "You don't have to wait for an invitation."

Caleb rolled his shoulders. "Grady sent me up to let you know the new horses are here. They're unloading them now, if you want to come look." His gaze roved around the office as the muscles in his jaw bunched. He kneaded the hat brim nervously.

He got it. Caleb wasn't unsure about being around Pierce. The office brought back too many memories of their dad. Even the air still held a hint of his particular brand of aftershave and the scent of boot polish he used on his boots. He'd had to come to terms with his father's memories, too. It wasn't easy.

"Let's go." Pierce stood and grabbed his hat from the rack beside the door, then followed his brother out into the brisk morning air. The sun was bright, but the rays didn't hold the warmth of summer. Two days until October, and this promised to be a chilly winter.

"Did you see any you liked?" Pierce settled his pace to match his brother's. These mares and geldings were from the Chance Ranch, some his dad had ordered but were delayed in delivery. The mares were good stock for their herd while the geldings were trained cutting horses.

"They're pretty fine." Caleb glanced at him. He hadn't shaved this morning and the scruff covering his jaw gave him a rugged appearance. He tipped his hat so the sun didn't get in his eyes. "I like one mare a lot. A couple of the geldings look like they have spirit, but Grady says they're all well-trained. I guess he went with Dad to look them over before they purchased them."

Pierce almost stopped in his tracks. That was more words than he'd heard his brother speak since coming home. Other than when he read to Kianna, and that didn't count as conversation.

"Sounds good. How many are there again?" He hadn't looked at the bill of sale since Grady first showed it to him a few weeks ago.

"Eight mares and six geldings. Grady said Dad wanted one stallion, but they were all sold. He got AI rights to one of the better stallions though, so that should help."

Artificial-insemination rights were the best way to ensure your stock could improve without having to purchase a stallion. Pierce had seen the listing on the particular horse they had AI rights to. He was an impressive beast, with the broad chest of a quarter horse, but also the stamina and agility of a mustang. Perfect for their needs.

The horses were milling in one of the larger corrals. Grady shook hands with the driver, and the man climbed into the cab and fired up his truck to growl down the newly smoothed and graveled driveway.

Grady strode over to them. "What do you think?"

Pierce leaned his folded arms on the fence rail and studied the horses. They ranged from a darker bay to a buckskin and one palomino. He'd bet Caleb had his eye on the palomino. Her coat gleamed in the sunlight, and the set of her head and intelligence in her eyes said she'd be a good horse to ride.

"They look good." Pierce clapped Grady on the shoulder. "You and Dad picked some good ones. What are your plans for them?"

"Caleb and I were talking about this. He has some good

ideas." Grady nodded at Caleb, who stood on Pierce's other side.

Pierce turned to study his brother. He'd almost forgotten that their dad had been training Caleb to take over the ranch in case Pierce didn't come home. Had he been wrong in not immediately getting Caleb's view on ranch matters upon his return?

Giving him time to settle in and recover from whatever happened to him might have been a mistake. Hadn't Silvia said something like that yesterday when the subject of his siblings came up? That he needed to involve them more and make them feel needed.

He waited until Caleb looked at him. "Tell me your thoughts. What would you do with these horses?"

Silvia had just finished cleaning up after dinner when a knock sounded on the front door. Her pulse skipped a merry rhythm. During dinner, her dad told her Pierce was supposed to come by this evening. Was he here?

All day, she'd looked forward to seeing him. He hadn't been at the cookhouse when she'd made her lunch delivery, but his truck was in the driveway. She'd swallowed her disappointment and continued on after chatting with Grady about some new stock that arrived that morning. But all afternoon, her thoughts strayed to Pierce and that incredible kiss.

Last night, she'd posted to her blog about their hike, with the pictures of the deer and some of the beautiful wildflowers. She even added a bit about the fire that tore through the canyon years ago and how the devastation still left many hillsides barren of trees.

As she'd heated dinner, she'd opened up her blog to check the comments. Her readers had been asking about updates and her next adventure. It turned out they didn't enjoy hearing about a tame hike along an idyllic river and a few deer, no matter how beautiful the shots. They wanted heart-pounding danger, like what she and Keith excelled at in the past.

Losing her readership might be a killer for her book deal. The publishing house wanted her story because of the outreach she had through her blog. If she lost that connection, would they still want her? She didn't think so.

If the publishing house dropped her, all the time and work she'd put in with Keith and Steven would be lost. They'd be forgotten. Their story left untold. How could she allow that to happen?

Her heart had been so heavy during dinner that she'd barely touched her meal. Her father carried the conversation, talking about how he built her dollhouse and the advice he had for Pierce. What was she doing here? She needed to get back on the road, travel to the next remote location and finish the chapters of the book. But doing so would disappoint her father and Pierce—the two men who meant most to her.

What if Pierce didn't understand? How could he? He'd never really understood her need for travel when she'd been younger. And though she believed him now, when he said he'd joined the army to prove to her he was ready to leave the ranch, would he really be amenable to her travels this time? Promising to come back seemed like an empty offering. What if the trips took longer than expected? What if she didn't make it back?

What if she ended up like Keith and Steven and her daughter?

She wiped her hands on a towel as the knock sounded again. "I've got it, Dad." Her legs felt like lead weights as she approached the door and swung it open. Pierce and Caleb stood on the porch. She raised her eyebrows as she studied Pierce's youngest brother. Caleb had grown up. His hollowed cheeks and shadowed eyes held some sort of pain she couldn't identify, but he looked good. Good enough to set the younger women's hearts fluttering.

"Caleb, good to see you. You, too, Pierce. Come on in." She stepped back to let them pass. "Dad's in the living room waiting for you."

Pierce stopped beside her, his scent of leather and horses washing over her. His eyes held a promise that broke her heart. She'd have to talk to him before he left tonight and tell him there wasn't anything between them. There couldn't be. Not now. Maybe never.

She wanted to collapse in a heap on the floor. Why did her life have to be so difficult? Her wants and needs were simple, so why were they always being denied?

The two Forester men continued on to the living room while she returned to the kitchen to put on a pot of decaf coffee. Pierce and Caleb probably drank regular, but her dad would be up more at night than usual if he had caffeine.

She carried in mugs to her father and Pierce, knowing they both liked it black. "Caleb, coffee?"

"Yes, please. Just black." His crooked smile gave him the look of a lost puppy. She wondered if that accounted for the dazed look in Tilly's eyes when they'd picked her up to take her home after their hike.

She brought coffee for herself with her favorite flavored creamer and handed Caleb his before sinking into a chair to listen to the men plan the dollhouse construction. She hadn't seen her father this invested in something since she'd returned home. *Please let this help him heal. I have to leave soon.*

"This is the list of materials you'll need." Her father pointed a shaky finger at the drawings they'd spread out on the coffee table.

Pierce leaned forward, reading off the list. "Did you use

all new materials? I'm considering using some repurposed wood. I'll make sure it's in good shape and treat it."

"I used some repurposed wood." Her dad nodded. "In fact, for the furniture, I used scraps of the wood from the exterior. You can save a lot that way."

"Do you have designs for the furniture, or did you just wing it?" Caleb scooted his chair closer and leaned over to view the drawing.

"I found a lot of those and copied them on the second page." Her father tried to separate the pages, but his fingers didn't want to obey. Caleb reached over to help and lifted off the top page to show one with several small drawings of tables, chairs, beds and cabinetry. Each one had dimensions and materials listed beside it.

Silvia's mind blanked. She had no idea her father had such talent in this area. As a young girl, she'd enjoyed the house. She'd spent hours playing with it. Not once had she considered how her father had built the house or the work done to figure everything out. New respect for him and her mom filled her. Her mom had hand-stitched the blankets, tiny napkins and dish towels. She'd even used lace to make curtains for the windows.

As Caleb and her dad continued to talk about working with tiny bits of material to make the small inner components of the house, Pierce turned to look at her. His warm gaze told her he was thinking of the kiss again. Which had her remembering, too. Her face warmed, and she brought the coffee to her lips to avoid staring back at him.

"So, Pierce." Caleb drew his attention from her and Silvia breathed a sigh. Caleb tapped on the pages of diagrams. "How about you work on the structure and I'll do the inner pieces? We can talk about what is important to get done for Christmas and go from there."

Pierce turned to her dad. "Do you think we have a chance of getting this finished by Christmas? It looks like a lot of work."

"You should be able to do the basics if you have the right tools." Her dad frowned and nodded. "The nice thing about a project like this is, it provides gifts for the next few years. You give her the house this Christmas and for her next birthday, you add something to the inside. Beds or tables. A piano. Some things you'll have to purchase, but there are places to find miniature items. If she likes cats or dogs, you can include those."

They talked a little longer until her dad's words slurred a bit, and his eyes drooped. Pierce rolled up the plans and put a rubber band around them to hold them in place. "Thanks, Pete. This is amazing. I'll take good care of these."

He handed the drawings to Caleb as her father shuffled off to his bedroom. "I'll meet you at the truck."

Caleb nodded at Silvia and headed out, leaving her alone with Pierce—the last place she wanted to be right now.

"Hey, how was your day?" Pierce drew close, his hands grasping hers. Silvia's heart ached so badly she wanted to pass out and not feel anymore. He ran his hands up her arms to her shoulders, his gaze intense. "What's wrong?"

She fumbled with her phone, almost dropping it on the floor. "Look at this." She held up the blog-post comments for him to read.

Pierce squinted at the screen. "What am I looking at?"

She held the phone closer to him. "All the negative comments from the posting on the hike we took. My readers expect more excitement than seeing a few deer." She closed her eyes as hurt flashed across his face.

"Why do you care what your readers like? Are you living your life for them or for you?"

She stared at Pierce. How could he ask something like that? "This is my job. I make my living this way. My following generates ad revenue, due to the premium subscribers I have. Sponsors provided gear for our travels and sometimes travel destinations, even my book deal. If my audience isn't happy with my content, I'll lose those sponsors and maybe even my book deal."

She almost grabbed him by the shirt to shake some understanding into him. "That's why I have to leave."

Chapter Seventeen

The look on Pierce's face when he realized how people had reacted to her new post and what it meant for them had kept Silvia awake for the past few nights. She'd slogged through work every day hoping to catch a glimpse of him when she did the delivery at Forester Ranch or when she took Kianna home. Nothing. He'd been avoiding her as if he'd rejoined the service and jetted off to parts unknown.

Wasn't that what she planned to do, though? She'd already looked into booking a flight for her next trip and arranging the equipment needed. Keith had planned for them to head to Peru to do paragliding for their next trip, which was why he and Steven were practicing the day they died. Just the thought of paragliding made her stomach pitch, but with winter approaching she'd considered trips to South America that would appeal to her followers and be something she and Keith hadn't done.

White-water rafting in Chile was on the list. She loved shooting dangerous rapids. The heart-pounding thrill. Being tossed around and in danger of hidden rocks, having the solid skills needed to avoid injury or death while challenging nature at its strongest. She and Keith had both become experts at class V rapids, and Chile's Futaleufú River was one of the best in the world for the thrill she sought.

Keith had considered several other South American options, and she'd been reading through his notes. Diving with sharks, skydiving—but they'd done that before in Europe. Mountain biking down a steep volcano sounded interesting, but she'd have to brush up on her mountain-biking skills. Climbing an ice mountain in Peru or sandboarding in the Atacama Desert were high on her list. Sandboarding, hmm. A pang twisted her heart at the memory of Steven wanting to try this.

These sounded intriguing and she would have been excited to go…once upon a time. But to go by herself didn't have the same allure. She and Keith had encouraged one another during the hard times. He'd been so good at understanding when she reached her limit and he'd back off or give her the perfect incentive she needed to pull through and finish.

How would she manage on her own? How would she keep her thoughts from constantly going to the loss of her family?

To the loss of Pierce?

She sat in the office at the restaurant and let the tears come. Losing so much left her bereft for months, and she still struggled to make it through some days. Now, she faced losing everything that mattered again. She'd made a promise. Given her word. Had people depending on her. So she had no choice.

A sharp rap on the office door stiffened her spine. She grabbed a tissue, wiped her face and blew her nose. "Come in."

Tilly rushed in, her hands twisting in her long T-shirt. "Jeanne's hurt. Burned at the stove."

Silvia pushed up from the desk, her worries disappearing. "Where is she? Did you call the paramedics?"

They ran down the hallway to the kitchen. Midafternoon meant fewer customers and less activity in the kitchen. They would be prepping for the dinner rush. How did Jeanne get burned doing that? *Thank You, God, that Kianna isn't here today.*

Her head cook sat on a stool near the back door cradling her arm. Tears swam in her eyes, and her face was as white as an apron. "I'm sorry." She pressed her lips together in a thin line and didn't move.

"What happened?" Silvia kneeled before her. The other helpers in the kitchen hovered behind them.

"I was carrying a couple of pans to the sink and stumbled on something. Lost my balance and fell. My arm landed on the stovetop." Tears leaked from Jeanne's eyes. Her shaky admission ended on a hiccupped sob.

"Let me see." Silvia lifted the cool towel draped over Jeanne's arm. The older woman hissed but didn't pull away. The skin had blistered, and the blisters had already broken. This wasn't just a slight burn. She'd need attention now.

"Did anyone call the paramedics?" She looked around. She'd asked Tilly earlier but hadn't waited to hear her response. A siren in the distance and a nod from Tilly told her the answer.

"Jeanne, we're going to let them look at you and take you to the hospital." Silvia eased the wet towel back down across the burn.

"But who will do the cooking?" Jeanne tried to stand, gasped and sat back down.

"I'll call Lonnie. I know it's his day off, but if he can't come in for a couple hours during the dinner rush, I'll cover it. You know I can do it." She kept her tone firm as she spoke.

Tilly opened the back door and motioned for the paramedics to come inside. Silvia stepped back, giving them space.

While they worked, she turned to the others in the kitchen. "Tilly, I want you to take charge in the dining room. Seat people and take orders, as usual. You know what to do."

She turned to the two kitchen helpers. They were both fairly new, and she blanked on their names. All she could see was the burn on Jeanne's arm. "I want you to do the prep work for dinner. You know how to do that, right?" They both nodded, and she breathed out, easing the tension in her shoulders. "Make sure you don't get in the way here, but get as much done as you can. I'll call Lonnie and take care of any orders that come in the meantime."

They all rushed off to do as she'd said. She turned back to Jeanne. The paramedics were bringing in a stretcher for her take her to the local hospital.

"Jeanne, I'll be by to see you as soon as I can. Is there someone you want me to call?" She grasped the woman's good hand.

Jeanne shook her head. "My daughter is back east right now. I'll be fine."

"I'll bring Dad by to see you. He won't rest until I do. You know that, right?"

The tears in Jeanne's eyes as she nodded made Silvia's eyes burn. As soon as they'd loaded Jeanne in the ambulance, Silvia rushed to the office to call Lonnie and prayed he'd be in town and able to come in.

The next few hours flew by and dragged at the same time. She called her dad to tell him she'd be late and to make a sandwich from the fixings in the refrigerator. He begged her to take him to the hospital, but she had no time to leave the restaurant.

Tilly poked her head through the kitchen door not long after Lonnie arrived. "Silvia, someone wants to talk to you."

Lonnie nodded at her and she pushed through the door to find Pierce waiting at the register. Their eyes met and a rush of relief coursed through her before she could stop it. "Pierce. How can I help you?"

"I heard what happened to Jeanne. I came by to pick up food to take to your dad. If you're going to be here, I can sit with him."

She pressed a hand to her chest. She hadn't expected such kindness after the blow she'd dealt him. Swallowing hard, she nodded. "That would be wonderful. Give me a few minutes and I'll have a meal ready for him. Would you like me to make one for you, too?"

Pierce's smile melted her heart. "I already ate with Mom and Kianna, but thanks."

A few minutes later she handed him the bag of food and watched him walk out the door. Was giving this up what she really wanted to do?

She stopped by the hospital on her way home, but it was past visiting hours. "Is she in a room? Is she going to be okay?"

"Let me see." The white-haired woman at the information desk checked her screen. "You're Silvia Rowland? Pete Durham's daughter?" The woman smiled at her. "Jeanne made sure you would receive an update. She's resting and will stay with us tonight so we can keep an eye on her. You can see her in the morning."

Silvia nodded and headed home, so unfocused she drove onto the shoulder at one point. She was tired, hungry because she'd forgotten to eat and emotionally drained. Her world was still spinning out of control and she wanted only one thing.

Well, two, to be exact.

She wanted—no, needed—to spend some time in prayer. To find out what God wanted of her.

And she needed Pierce. A need that would never be fulfilled.

Pierce rubbed his tired eyes. He'd been staring at this computer screen way too long, and his body required about twenty-four hours of sleep, since he'd lost some staying with Pete last night until Silvia returned home. Those stupid missing cows still troubled him. His dad had been meticulous in his recordkeeping until those cows came along. Now, it seemed like a whole chunk of information was missing. Even with the hidden files he'd found, there wasn't enough.

The big mystery, and one he hadn't broached with Grady, was why the Department of Agriculture hadn't investigated. Someone always contacted them on any suspected livestock thievery. While he knew that his dad hadn't wanted to accuse Mason without solid proof, in all the paperwork, he hadn't found any information indicating that his dad even contacted the authorities to report the missing cattle.

Part of him wanted to climb into his truck and go confront Mason. The man had issues and treated everyone as if they were beneath him. Pierce did not like dealing with him, and his dad had felt the same. Still, sitting around wondering and not finding the evidence he needed was driving him crazy.

Just tonight, he'd snapped at Kianna for a silly game she was playing. He wanted her in bed and she was still wound up from the dessert his mom fed her. Chocolate and Kianna didn't mix. Normally, he'd be patient, but this time the thought of figuring out this problem weighed so heavily that he'd barked at her to stop fooling around and get in bed. It wasn't his words as much as his tone of voice.

He dropped his head on his arms and groaned. The way her little face crumpled would keep him awake at night. She'd sobbed, calling for her mother. She didn't want him to hold her or tuck her in. He'd have to figure out a way to make this up to her. To let her know he loved her even when he was grumpy.

Voices outside preceded the sound of shoes scraping on

the grate outside the outer door. After a brief knock, Caleb poked his head inside. "Got some time? We need to talk."

"Come on in." Pierce motioned to the coffee he'd just finished brewing. "Grab some coffee and a chair."

Caleb and Grady slipped inside and closed out the breeze that held the chill of the mountain air. The coming rain might bring an early snow.

When the other men had finally settled, Pierce leaned back in his chair and cradled his coffee cup, studying the pair. "So...what's up?"

"We need to talk about the missing cattle." Caleb leaned forward, resting his elbows on his knees, hands wrapped around his cup. Pierce wondered if his brother had read his mind. He glanced at Grady, then back to Pierce. "Have you found anything?"

"No. And I have questions." Pierce looked at Grady. "Why can't I find any evidence that the Department of Ag was called in? There should at least be a report somewhere, but I've gone through everything in the files and on the computer. Nothing."

Grady leaned back in his chair, bringing one ankle up to rest on his knee. He took a sip of the hot brew. "I don't believe your dad called them. Did he, Caleb?"

Caleb shook his head. "No, he didn't." His posture sagged as if he had more to say but wanted to keep quiet. What was going on here?

Pierce set his mug on the desk. "Well, I need to know why. Why would Dad buy these big-priced animals and then not report them missing? I've counted one hundred fifty-four missing cattle. I found a file to that effect. But there's nothing else. No paper trail on evidence or reports or money."

A muscle ticked in his jaw. How was he supposed to run a ranch when he didn't have the entire story? When everyone around him was keeping secrets? He even suspected his mom of knowing something about the cattle that she hadn't shared.

Did they want him to fail? Was this some sort of test? A trial by fire, or one weighted against him as a punishment for being gone so long? If so, maybe he should just pack up Kianna and take off for parts unknown.

He had friends who wanted him to join them in a security and protection business. His time in spec ops qualified him for that kind of work, and he'd be good at it.

But his dad had wanted him to run the ranch, and truth be told, he wanted it, too—had for most of his life. His father left this spread to him with the idea he would keep it going and leave it for the next generation of Foresters. He refused to fail his dad, even if everyone stood in his way. Even if it meant selling off some of the land to get out of debt.

Even if Silvia left Ashville and never returned, taking his heart with her.

At that thought, he closed his eyes and groaned a prayer. He had no words, but God understood his needs. Pierce had to trust Him to provide what was necessary and to show him what to do next.

He slapped his palms on his legs, ignoring the sting. Caleb and Grady both jumped. He glared at them with his best I'm-in-charge military face. "I need to know what you know. Now! This ranch is failing—barely making ends meet—and we'll lose it if I don't turn things around. Talk to me."

The pair glanced at each other. Caleb nodded his head. His shoulders hunched forward before he met Pierce's gaze. "This is all my fault. Grady didn't know anything until I talked to him yesterday. He said I needed to talk to you. And he's right."

"Your fault how?" Pierce didn't say any of the usual niceties. He needed facts and truth. If his brother was uncomfortable, so be it.

"When Dad bought those cattle, he overextended to get them. He had a plan to get the money back, plus extra. He put me in charge of his plan." The coffee in Caleb's hands came close to spilling as it rippled in the cup.

"What plan?" Pierce asked, and Grady patted Caleb on the shoulder.

"He purchased those cattle for a steal, but he didn't intend to keep them all. He slated twenty head of the cows to be sold at auction, which would make up for the debt plus a little. Then we'd have the others to raise more calves to sell the next spring."

Caleb leaned down and set his mug on the floor. He rubbed his palms on his jeans, keeping his gaze down. His mouth opened and closed, as if the words were stuck in his throat.

"Caleb, what happened? Just tell me." Pierce attempted to tone down his glare, but from the look on Caleb's face, he failed.

"I got in some trouble. With some guys who were out to get revenge. Because of the accident. And other things." Caleb's eyes shone in the low light of the room. "They threatened to kill me if I didn't get the money I owed them. Dad found out. He sold all those cattle to pay that debt and gave me what was left to leave town. He didn't trust them to not come after me, anyway."

A kick from a mule wouldn't hurt any worse. Pierce stared at his brother. "Why didn't Dad put that in the records?"

"Maybe I can answer that." Grady put down his empty cup and crossed his arms. "My guess is, he worried people wouldn't understand or that the men who wanted revenge on Caleb would catch wind of it. Like they'd want the money or something. He made up the story about the cattle disappearing, but I don't think he believed anyone would suspect Mason. I believe he planned to make it right, but then he got sick and died before he had the chance." He paused, frowning. "Your dad wasn't thinking clearly at the time."

Pierce nodded. His body felt so heavy that if he fell in a lake, he'd sink to the bottom and drown. So Chet Mason had done nothing wrong. Caleb had gotten into a bad situation, and his father had tried to help. But he'd been culpable, too, by not documenting anything. It struck him that the FSS computer file didn't stand for Forester Stolen Stock but for Forester Stock Sold.

He eyed Caleb. "Does this have to do with why you were in jail?"

Caleb paled a little more and shook his head. "No. Nothing. I promise."

"Does Mom know about this?"

Caleb shifted in his chair. "Maybe. Dad didn't keep anything from her. But he also protected her, so who knows?"

He trusted his brother. He wanted him to confess everything, but maybe it was still too painful. Just like Silvia taking so long to talk about losing her baby girl. Maybe in time Caleb would trust him with the whole truth.

Pierce's pulled his thoughts back to their conversation and his gut clenched at all the negative thoughts he'd had about their neighbor. What kind of rancher was he? Maybe he should sell after all, travel the world with Silvia instead of pretending to be a rancher.

And that led to thoughts of how she was coping since Jeanne's accident. Thoughts of how much he wanted to be there for her, if only she'd let him.

Chapter Eighteen

It took Pierce two days to track down Quinn and Ashlyn to set up a time for a Zoom conference. He'd confronted his mom and sat her down with Caleb, and they hashed out what had happened and what to do about the ranch. The finances were in terrible shape, and they needed a quick way to make some cash, plus a long-term plan.

Caleb had gone to get their mom and Kianna while Pierce finished making coffee and setting everything up for their meeting. He prayed the twins would be on board with helping. Or at least care about their home and their mother enough to give input.

He still had several minutes until the call. He pulled out his phone and called Silvia. She answered on the first ring.

"Hey." She sounded a bit breathless, and his heart thumped.

"Hey. I thought I'd call and check on Jeanne." He listened as she filled him in on the older woman's progress. Then he told her about what he'd discovered about the supposedly stolen cows.

"Wow, that's unexpected." A chair creaked and he pictured her in the office at the Chuckwagon.

"Listen, Silvia, I need to ask…" Pierce closed his eyes and sent up a prayer for the right words. "What are your plans? Do you want to go back to the life you shared with your husband, to the extreme adventures?"

"Why do you ask?" A chill entered her voice.

"Because you seem to enjoy being here. You're good at running the restaurant. You fit in here." He almost blurted out that she fit with him.

Silence followed. He started to say something, but just let the quiet hang, letting her take the lead. She blew out a breath. "Pierce, I can't give you a definite answer. But I can admit to you that I'm torn. I have responsibilities, promises I made, plans for the future." She sniffed.

He heard his family coming. "Just think about it. Pray about your decision. I'll pray, too." Should he say how much he wanted her to stay? No, she'd have to be clueless to miss how he felt. He said his good-night and ended the call.

"We're here." Kianna bounced into the room toting a bag full of dolls and stuffed animals. She headed to the corner, where he'd spread out a blanket over two chairs to make her a little fort to play in. She'd forgiven him for his grumpiness the other night. Kids were always so forgiving.

He smiled as she climbed inside the little fort and then rushed out to give him a hug before disappearing again. His mom settled in the chair closest to where Kianna played, as they'd agreed. She would keep his daughter distracted while he and Caleb talked to their siblings.

"Is it time?" Caleb poured coffee for Mom and himself before settling in a chair that squeaked when he leaned back.

"Two minutes. I'll go ahead and open the room in case they're early." Pierce logged in and turned the monitor to have all three of them on the screen.

A minute later, Quinn and Ashlyn appeared on the screen, sitting close together. They shared a two-bedroom apartment somewhere in the LA area. Pierce had never been there.

"Quinn, Ashlyn, it's good to see you." He smiled. He hadn't seen them in a couple of years apart from watching their show when he could. He'd never understand how they ended up with their own reality TV show documenting their lives as twins, but it seemed to suit them. They were often at odds, but were fun to watch and had quite a following.

"Good to see you, Pierce." Ashlyn twisted the ends of her reddish-blond hair. She had a round face that gave her that girl-next-door look that appealed to her audience.

"Pierce. Tired of the ranch already?" Quinn's jab hurt. His brother had meant it to hurt. He usually did. "Since you couldn't even be bothered to come for Dad's funeral."

Pierce glanced at his mom. He knew she understood, but he still saw the hurt that shone in her eyes. He owed his family the truth. "I couldn't come." He cleared his throat. "I was in Germany, laid up in a hospital. Stepped in the way of some bullets."

Stunned quiet filled the room, followed by a plethora of questions, most of which he couldn't answer because of confidentiality. At least Quinn wasn't so openly antagonistic now, and the hurt had disappeared from his mom's eyes.

"What's this meeting about?" Quinn asked when the conversation slowed. "Are you finally selling the ranch?"

Their mom gasped. "What? You want to sell the ranch?" She hadn't been privy to the twins' earlier assertion that they should sell the ranch and divide the proceeds among them.

"No. We are not selling the ranch." Pierce's tone hardened. "That's not what Dad wanted." He continued laying out the problems they were having, with input from Caleb and his mom. Quinn and Ashlyn kept quiet, their glances at each other and their expressions showing they didn't like this at all.

"If the ranch is in debt, why don't you just get rid of it? You can pay off the debt and use the rest to find a decent place for Mom." Quinn stood up and walked back and forth in the room, coming in and out of camera range.

"This is my home." His mom was near tears. Her lower lip trembled. "I almost came to terms with selling to Chet Mason when I had no other choices but… I don't think I can go through that again."

"Mom, we're keeping the ranch." Pierce took her hand in his and gave a gentle squeeze.

They talked about options for the rest of the time they had in the meeting. No conclusions were made, but Pierce had some ideas he wanted to discuss with Caleb.

The minutes were counting down when Pierce held up a hand to stop a back-and-forth between the twins and Caleb. "I'd like the two of you to consider coming home for a few days. We could hash this out and make a plan."

Quinn shook his head. "We don't have the time. We have more shows to tape and some appearances we can't miss."

"Just for a weekend. Or a couple of days during the week." He didn't understand their lack of concern for their mother and the family home.

Quinn started to speak, but Ashlyn put her hand on his arm. "We'll look at our schedule and discuss it. No promises."

"Okay. Thank you." Pierce said his goodbyes, as did everyone else. He clicked out of the program and shut down the computer. He had to get away for a few minutes. To somewhere.

"What do you say we load up and go to the Chuckwagon for dinner?"

"Yay! Miss Silvy!" Kianna popped her head out of the tent.

"I don't know if she'll be there this late." Pierce's heart thumped at the thought of seeing her.

"From what I hear, she's been running the restaurant by herself. Pete says she's exhausted and losing weight. He's pretty upset."

"Get ready. We're heading to town in twenty minutes." Pierce grabbed Kianna's hand, heading to her room.

"Hey. Look at you lying around doing nothing. I never thought I'd see the day. Is this a hospital or a five-star hotel?" Silvia leaned down to give Jeanne a kiss on the forehead. The older woman's brow knit with pain, but she managed a wan smile.

"I'm telling you I want to overhaul the kitchen in this place. You should try the food." She grimaced. "I might starve to death before I get out of here."

Silvia pulled a chair next to the bed and sat down. She wrapped her arms around her overlarge purse and lowered her voice to a conspiratorial whisper. "If you don't rat me out, I may have something that will save your life." She gave an exaggerated glance at the door before extracting a bag from the Chuckwagon. She set the purse on the floor and opened the bag. The scents of roast beef and fresh cookies filled the room.

"Quick. Close the door." Jeanne nodded toward the hallway. "Those nurses have noses that could catch the scent of cookies a mile away. They'll claim I'm too sick and confiscate them."

Silvia chuckled. "Actually, I cleared the food with them before bringing it in here. And I left them with their own cookies at the desk. I think they're too busy eating to care about what you have."

When the midafternoon slump hit the restaurant, Silvia had taken a few minutes to come by the hospital in Springerville to see Jeanne. The cook's arm had become infected, so she had to stay longer. Silvia brought her some familiar food to cheer her up.

"Do you want to eat this now or save it for dinnertime?" She held up the roast beef sandwich that was Jeanne's favorite.

"Give me half now. And a cookie. I'll save the rest for later." Jeanne bit into the rosemary bread filled with meat, cheese, veggies and green chilis, and moaned. "I didn't eat but about two bites of lunch. I couldn't even tell what they were trying to poison me with. And don't get me started on breakfast. Those eggs must have been laid by alien chickens from Mars." She shuddered and took another bite.

"I've been worried about chickens from Mars. Do you think they came on a spaceship or maybe a space egg?" Silvia bit her lip, knowing Jeanne didn't believe in aliens any more than she did. It was an old joke between them. If anything went wrong, aliens from Mars caused it.

Jeanne relaxed back in the bed and laughed. Her color was better, so the company helped. Maybe Silvia could bring her dad to visit tomorrow. If she figured out how to keep the restaurant going while taking the time to drive to her place, the hospital and back. If her dad agreed to go to the restaurant afterward with her, that might work.

"When are you attempting to escape this joint?" Silvia pulled a cookie from the bag and broke off a bite.

"Are you eating my cookies? You're as bad as those nurses." Jeanne narrowed her eyes.

Silvia grinned and took another bite. "I came from the source. Be nice and I'll bring more for you tomorrow."

"Turns out, I can leave tomorrow. If I have someone to babysit me." Jeanne laughed. "I told the doctor Bob lives with me and can take care of me."

"Does the doctor know Bob is your cat?" Silvia almost snorted out cookie crumbs.

"No, he doesn't. And don't you tell him." Jeanne took another bite of her sandwich.

"Well, you're not going home with just Bob there. I'll grab up Bob, and the two of you can come to our house to stay. I'll talk to your doctor and see what you need."

"Pete doesn't need me underfoot."

"My dad will love having you there. Especially if he gets to boss you around." Silvia winked at Jeanne and glanced at her watch. "I have to go. Lonnie is holding the fort, but he'll need help."

"Silvia." Jeanne set down her sandwich on the wrapper. "Take care of yourself. You're doing too much."

"I'll be fine." Silvia stood and brushed another kiss on Jeanne's forehead.

"I mean it." Jeanne caught her hand. "You need to consider what's best for you and do that. Pray. Stop doing so much for others and take time to line your life up with God's will."

Her friend wasn't talking about living arrangements or working at the restaurant anymore. Silvia's throat clogged, and she nodded, unable to speak. She waved goodbye and left before she fell on the floor in a sobbing heap.

The past few days had been too stressful. She had trouble keeping up with everything. Marissa had called to say Catherine wanted more chapters now, not next week. And, she encouraged Silvia to write about Keith and Steven again, but that wasn't an option.

With the extra work, Silvia had been too exhausted when she returned home at night to do more than shower and climb into bed...where she thought about Pierce instead of getting much needed sleep.

Back at the restaurant, she slipped on an apron and washed up, ready to help.

"Good thing you're back," Lonnie called from across the kitchen. "We have a big party coming in an hour. They're having a birthday party, so we reserved the back room for them. We'll need all hands on deck to make this work."

Silvia nodded and settled into the rhythm of prepping and helping in the dining room when needed. She'd learned all aspects of the work as a teen, and now, each job felt comfortable and familiar.

She was at the register ringing up the large party when Pierce walked in with his mom, Caleb and Kianna. She lost her train of thought and had to clear the register and start over. Pierce nodded at her as they followed Tilly to a booth by the windows.

Why did he have to be so handsome? And so kind? And so thoughtful? And so... The list was long. Why did her heart have to gallop when he walked in the door?

She finished with the tab and smoothed her apron as the customers walked outside. It was dark, and the lights shone in the parking area. The scent of rain whooshed in on the evening air.

Two more couples approached, ready to pay their bills. She tried to focus on ringing them up and not noticing how Pierce sat in the booth facing her, his focus intent. Her hands shook a little as she handed the last customer their change and they left.

Pierce stood, heading her way with his graceful stride, and her knees wobbled. He stopped in front of the register. "Can we talk?"

She glanced outside. Their big party hadn't arrived yet, and most people already had their food. "For a few minutes. Come back to the office."

She sat behind the desk and he took the chair across from her.

"How are you doing?" Pierce's gaze held steady on her.

"I hear you're running the restaurant and still doing the deliveries."

"Thanks for asking Caleb to pick up Kianna in my place," she said, avoiding the question. "Not that watching Kianna was ever a hardship." She almost rested her head on the back of the chair but didn't want to fall asleep. "I'm getting by."

"Have you considered what we talked about?" He might as well have asked if she'd considered him. Which she had—every night before she fell asleep.

She rubbed her eyes and sighed. "I may be good at running the Chuckwagon, but I'm not sure this is my calling." Leaning forward, she rested her elbows on the desk. "I have this duty to my followers, my agent, my editor—but mostly to my family that died. Pierce, I gave my word at their grave sites that I'd continue the adventures, that I'd finish the book. How can I go back on my word?"

The sadness in his gaze tore at her.

"What about, I don't know…doing some climbing here? Or some skiing in another month or two when there's snow?"

"My followers want danger, not something tame. Keith and I hit a certain level and our followers have expectations." She pushed back from the desk. "I have to get back to work. We have a big party coming in."

Pierce stood and grabbed her hands. He pulled her into a hug that felt so right her breath stuttered as she stared up at him. He gave a soft smile. "Keep praying. Consider what God wants, not what your followers want."

Chapter Nineteen

Silvia dragged through the next week. Jeanne was out of the hospital, ensconced at the house with Pete, and was healing pretty fast. Her dad enjoyed the company during the day and had been progressing some with his physical abilities. He still had a long way to go to help at the restaurant, but every step forward was an encouragement.

The long hours at the Chuckwagon and coming home to work on her book were wearing on Silvia. Editing chapters proved much harder than writing them. Or maybe just more tedious. She liked the thrill of getting the adventure down on the page, but the polishing wasn't as much fun.

One more chapter to finish, and then the final three adventures to do and to write about unless Marissa's suggestion was accepted. She'd followed Marissa's advice and written three chapters on earlier treks she and Keith had experienced, but she didn't see their readers or the publisher being interested in the milder sports, where they'd been learning and practicing.

Tomorrow, she would try to finish up and send everything to Marissa. Then she'd make a final decision about when and where to go and what to do next.

She'd prayed hard the past week, expecting God to make the path forward clear, but He hadn't. Why didn't He just text her or send a road map? Anything so His will was clear.

After climbing out of bed, she got ready for the day. The

sun wasn't up yet when she padded down to the kitchen to find her dad measuring coffee into the pot. This was his newest accomplishment, and her chest filled with warmth watching him. It was almost like waking early as a young girl and finding him in the kitchen, starting coffee and then pancakes.

"Good morning." He glanced her way and smiled. Some of the coffee grounds were scattered across the counter.

"Good morning. Do you have a spare IV line so I can set up a drip of that coffee?" She winked at him. The two of them had always shared a love of the caffeinated brew, while her mom had preferred tea.

He finished the process and pushed the button to start the machine. When he faced her with a look of satisfaction on his face, she had to smile. "Nice job, Dad."

"Wait 'til you taste it. Might be so strong it'll make your hair curly." He grinned, and they both laughed. Her mom used to tell her coffee would turn her hair curly, and back then Silvia did not want curls. Now, she wouldn't mind a few.

"I made pancake batter." Her dad nodded at a covered bowl on the counter. She glanced around, expecting a mess, but didn't see any. He was truly improving. A blessing. Not just because he would soon be self-sufficient, but because he would be happier if he returned to some semblance of his former life.

"I'll start cooking. Is Jeanne still asleep?" Silvia grabbed the griddle from the cabinet by the stove, then propped it over two burners.

"She is." Her dad opened the refrigerator and handed her a package of bacon and a dozen eggs. She lifted her eyebrows. "Hungry this morning?"

"Yes." He headed for the doorway. "While you cook, I'll get dressed. I'm going with you."

She stared open-mouthed at his back. What brought this

on? Up to now, he had shown no interest in going to the restaurant, not even when his friends took him there after church.

Early hours at the restaurant were hectic and mindless. She
rushed from one job to the next, helping with the meals and
prepping for the box lunches. Her father talked with customers and then disappeared into the office and closed the door.

She had the lunches loaded up when she went to knock on
the office door. She opened it to see her father seated at the
desk perusing the books. He glanced up at her and smiled.

"I'm heading out to do the deliveries. Do you want me to
take you home? Or would you like to go on the run with me?"
She leaned against the doorframe, unable to stop the rush
spreading through her at the sight of her father right where he
belonged—in the office chair, books in front of him, tapping
a pencil on the desk. It couldn't get better than this.

He put the pencil in the LA Dodgers cup he'd used for
years to hold his pens and pencils and pushed back from the
desk. "I'll go with you. Then you can take me home on the
way back."

"Sounds good. I'll meet you in the car." Silvia whipped up
a couple of extra boxes while her dad made his way through
the dining area, greeting the few who were there midmorn-
ing for chats with friends or meetings.

Deliveries took longer than usual. By the time they reached
the Forester Ranch, they were way behind. Silvia zipped down
the driveway, glad Pierce had fixed the divots and added
gravel.

Grady waited outside the cookhouse along with a few of
the cowboys. Silvia nodded at them as she put the car in
Park. "They're probably starving because you have so many
friends."

"It's good for them to learn to wait." Her dad opened his
door to a chorus of enthusiastic greetings. The door to the

house clacked above the din, and Pierce strode in their direction. Silvia fumbled with the wagon and almost dropped it. She hadn't seen him since he talked to her at the restaurant, asking about Jeanne.

He hugged her dad and welcomed him, but barely spoke to her. She stuffed the hurt down deep. This was her own doing. She was the one who didn't want a relationship. Who wanted to leave. Who told him it would never work.

Had she been wrong?

"Let me take that." Grady grabbed the wagon handle and pulled the load of lunches to the building. Her dad and the cowboys followed, all except Pierce. His steady gaze rested on her. Silvia's stomach clenched and her legs refused to move.

Then he was in front of her, taking her hands in his. And his touch sent a thrill through her. *No. No. No. I can't feel anything for him.*

"Silvia, you look exhausted. How's Jeanne?"

She swallowed and dragged her gaze from his. "She's improving. She might even be back to work by next week." She stared at their clasped hands, needing to pull away but unable to make her hands obey.

He tugged her closer and wrapped his arms around her. "I've been praying for you—for all you have to do and for decisions you need to make."

Tears prickled her eyes. She relaxed into the hug. Why had God allowed them to go their separate ways? Why was she so locked into fulfilling the dreams she'd shared with Keith?

Pierce gave another squeeze before stepping back. Grady and her dad were making their slow way back, Grady pulling the wagon.

"Thanks." She forced the word from her constricted throat as Pierce studied her. "For the prayers. I've been praying, too."

On the drive to the house to take her dad home, he turned

to her. "I know you think you need to traipse all over the world again, but have you prayed about it? I'd like you to stay here. You've done a phenomenal job with the restaurant since Jeanne's been hurt."

"Dad, I've prayed so much I'd have calluses on my knees if I kneeled every time. I just don't know what God wants."

"Maybe you're telling Him what you want in life instead of leaving Him room to show you what He wants." He squeezed her shoulder as she turned into their lane. "Consider why you were doing what you were doing. Is the need to continue still there? Is there something else that God might want you to do instead?"

"I don't know what." Her throat clogged, and she swallowed hard.

"Maybe you're trying too hard to make someone else's dream come true." Her dad clicked open his door as the car stopped. He reached in the back and took the two box lunches labeled for him and Jeanne, then shut the door. She watched until he reached the front door and waved at her. She waved back, blinking to bring him into focus.

Maybe you're trying to make someone else's dream come true. Was she?

"What are you doing?" Caleb settled into the chair beside Pierce's and stared at the computer screen.

"Looking at my retirement fund. I set this up when I was in the service, and I've added to it regularly."

Caleb whistled. "I didn't realize the military paid that well. Maybe I should join."

"The military doesn't pay that well, but they cover what you need. If you're careful and make some wise investments, you can stash away a decent amount. Plus, I received hazard pay for some of the work I did." Pierce minimized the window and turned to his brother. "What's up?"

"Why are you looking at your retirement fund?" Caleb narrowed his eyes. "You're not thinking of cashing it in and using it to help the ranch, are you?"

Pierce ground his teeth together. He hadn't counted on anyone finding out. In the past week, he'd gone over every scenario to save the ranch, and this was the only viable option he'd come up with. "Maybe."

"Don't." Caleb barked out the word. "Save it for your kids, your family."

"Then do you have any ideas that might help?" Pierce stared out the window and watched Silvia drive up with the day's lunches. Her dad had come with her yesterday, but he wasn't with her today. Which meant Pierce didn't have an excuse to go out and be close to her. To torture himself was more like it.

"Quit staring at her and listen." Caleb's voice held a hint of aggravation. Pierce turned away from the window.

Caleb made a fist with his left hand and cracked the knuckles. "I've been looking into something a friend did in Montana. He built a hunting lodge on their ranch. Not too close to the house. It was kind of like a bed-and-breakfast, and they provided lunches the hunters could take with them for the day."

Pierce leaned forward to put his elbows on his knees. He'd never heard of this, but they had a lot of hunters in these mountains, usually in the cooler months. "Go on."

"He also has a couple of guys who know the area and they offer to guide hunters, especially those from out of state who don't know where to find the game. It's a lucrative business."

Caleb rubbed his palms up and down his jeans before settling back and crossing his arms. "You and I are both accomplished hunters in these mountains, or at least you used to be. We could do the guiding."

"What kind of money are we talking?"

Caleb named a figure that made Pierce's mouth drop open. He stared up at the ceiling as he processed the information. "That might be a long-term solution to help out, but we need something short-term that will raise money now. We'd have to build the lodge and get everything set up. It would be next year before we could even start to see an income."

"So let's sell a few of those cows. The ones dad bought from the Cranes. We still have about fifty head. Grady said we got top dollar for the calves. Take that amount and sell a few cows or some of our others. Enough to tide us over for the winter. When things are looking up, we can build the herd again." Caleb's blue eyes shone with enthusiasm as he spoke. Pierce pictured what his brother proposed and saw the merit.

"Okay. I'll take this into consideration. How about you look at the value of the cows and see if there is a buyer and how many we need to part with."

Caleb grinned and jumped to his feet. "I'll do that and let you know. I already did some research, so it shouldn't take long." He opened the door leading into the house. Their mom was just outside, her hand raised to knock.

"Mom." Pierce beckoned to her. "You don't have to knock."

She hugged Caleb in passing and stepped inside the office. "I didn't want to bother you if you were busy. Then I heard voices and wasn't sure if I should disturb you."

"You're always welcome. Have a seat. Coffee?" He glanced at the pot full of dark sludge that he'd made early that morning and forgotten to drink. "If you want coffee, I'll make fresh. I could use a cup, too."

The fresh coffee warmed him as he drank, chatting with his mom about Caleb's ideas and the logistics. Where they would put a hunting lodge. How big to build it. Whether to make one larger building or cabins.

"Here I am going on about Caleb's ideas. I didn't ask if you had a reason to come to the office. Is there something you need?" Pierce stood to refill his mug, but his mom shook her head and covered the top of hers.

"Can't I just come have a chat with my oldest without a reason?"

"You can." Pierce settled back in the leather chair, the same place his dad sat for years. He still didn't feel like he fit in his father's shoes, but he was trying hard.

"Well, it turns out you're right. I have something I want to talk to you about." She ran her thumb around the rim of her mug, her gaze lowered. Pierce's stomach knotted. He put his coffee on the desk and waited.

When his mom had something serious to talk about, she took her time getting ready. No way to rush her. You just had to wait her out and be prepared for something deeper than you wanted.

She looked up at him, her gaze intense, her expression serious. "I want to talk to you about Silvia. I've been talking with Pete, and we're both concerned about the two of you."

"Mom." He closed his eyes and dropped his head back. Faced her again. "Let Silvia and me work out what's between us. Which is nothing. She's leaving again and has no room for me in her life. She doesn't want to stay in Ashville."

"Have you asked her?"

"Asked her what?"

His mom let out a heavy sigh, as if he was the densest male in the history of the world. "Asked her to stay?"

"I suggested that she might want to," he said.

"Uh-huh. Have you told her how you feel about her? That you love her."

"Mom." He reared back in the chair, and the base squealed. "What makes you think I love her?"

"Pierce Forester, I'm your mother. You've loved that girl for years. I've watched you since you've been back, and you light up like a firework when she's around. Anyone could see it."

The sledgehammer of her words hit hard. Was she right? He didn't even have to ponder that question. He's always loved Silvia. But had everyone noticed? No, he'd hidden his feelings.

Had he hidden them too well? Had Silvia missed that what he felt for her was more than a passing infatuation? Did she realize the depth of his love for her?

What if she didn't? What if she was leaving because she didn't see a need to stay—because being around him without a relationship was as painful for her as it was for him?

A sudden urgency had him dropping his feet to the floor. "Mom, you are the best." He leaned forward to hug her. "I need to go."

"Wait." She reached into her pocket and pulled out a small box. Tears glittered in her eyes as she handed it to him. "I don't know if you're ready for this step, but when you are, you are welcome to use my rings. They're handed down from your great-grandmother."

Pierce flipped open the tiny box to see a glittering diamond surrounded by emeralds nestled next to the wedding band. For years, he'd seen these rings on his mom's hand. Heard the stories of his ancestors and how they came by the set.

"Thanks, Mom. We aren't at that point yet, but I appreciate the thought." He cleared his throat to ease the ache, snapped the box shut and shoved it in his pocket as he stood. While Silvia might not be at the point of considering marriage, he was. Mom's gesture touched his heart in a way words wouldn't. "Let me walk you back in. Then I have to go."

Chapter Twenty

His breath created a fog of white as Pierce stood on the porch the next morning watching the sky turn from indigo to an artist's array of pinks, oranges and blues. He blinked, trying to get moisture in eyes that had more sand than the Sahara. Numbness would be preferable to the ache of loss that compressed his chest this morning.

Silvia was gone. Oh, he didn't have confirmation yet, since Pete had been asleep when he reached the house last night. But Silvia's car was gone. He'd even driven to the Chuckwagon on the off chance she'd stayed extra late to work on something. Nothing. No one was there.

She was gone. Again.

The door creaked, and Caleb stepped out beside him, carrying two steaming mugs of coffee. "You look like a pack of coyotes dragged you through the hills last night. What's up?"

Pierce took the proffered cup and sipped the dark liquid. He opened his mouth to reply but had no words. He shrugged, swallowing against the ache in his throat.

"I heard you leave last night. I also heard what Mom told you. Did you see Silvia?" Caleb leaned back against the porch railing.

"No." He cleared his throat. "She's gone."

Caleb frowned. "Gone? How do you know? Did you talk to Pete?"

Pierce shook his head. "He was in bed. There wasn't any light in the house."

"So you're going to stand out here and freeze to death and mope based on an assumption? Didn't you learn anything in the military?"

"What do you mean?" Pierce tried to tone down his aggravation but failed.

"What about facts? Did the military send you on ops based on assumptions? They assumed insurgents were holding someone in a certain place, so they sent you in without being sure?" Caleb's mouth twisted in a sardonic smile. "I think they ascertained the facts before they dispatched the team. Am I right?"

He was. Absolutely right. What if Silvia had spent the night elsewhere with a friend or something? What if this was a lack of information again? What if she hadn't left? What if there was still time to convince her to stay? In Ashville.

With him.

He started to hand the mug to Caleb when he realized the hour. No way could he disturb Pete this early. He'd have to wait until later, when the older man would be awake and ready for company.

"Thanks. I'll head down and talk with Grady." His brain blanked on anything to do other than go after Silvia. To find her and plead his case to her.

"I'll come with you. I did some research last night on the cattle prices and buyers. Grady always has a good perspective and a lot of knowledge. He can weigh in. We can also get his take on the lodge idea." Caleb went down the steps before looking back at Pierce. "Coming?"

He took a long slug of coffee. Followed his brother as he headed for Grady's cabin. Admired the colorful sky even as the brightness of the display faded into morning.

"Hey, look there." Caleb paused and pointed across the road at the wide-open pastures. In the middle, a herd of elk was wading through the grass on their way to a higher ground.

Pierce stopped to watch their stately movements. Where deer were graceful and quick, elk walked with a regal stride that proclaimed their importance. Not that they weren't fast. When startled, they ran like the wind and were so beautiful they'd take your breath away.

"Come in." Grady's call had Caleb opening the door. The foreman was at his small stove, cooking up some eggs for his breakfast. "Hey. You want an egg sandwich? I have just enough to make you one."

"No thanks. We'll eat with Mom soon." Caleb pulled out a chair at the small table and sat. Pierce sat beside him.

Grady finished his cooking his breakfast, picked up the plate and sat down with them. "How can I help you? You're up early."

"We have some ideas to run by you." Pierce took over at Caleb's nod and filled in Grady on all they'd discussed the evening before. Grady ate and listened without comment before getting up to take his plate to the sink and fill everyone's coffee.

"That lodge idea is intriguing. Where would you put it?"

Caleb leaned forward and pulled a piece of paper from his pocket. He unfolded it to show a map of their ranch. The house and outbuildings were sketched in as squares, and arrows indicated directions to town and the surrounding ranches. The drawing was surprisingly detailed reminding Pierce of the days when Caleb constantly had a pencil and paper for his artwork.

"I'd put the lodge here." He gestured at a section of land that was only a couple of miles from Ashville. "The hunters would have easy access to town, where they could get supplies or meals, even have a relaxing night out if they chose to."

"Oh, the Ashville nightlife." Grady snorted, and they all laughed. Ashville rolled up the sidewalks—the few they had—by ten at night. For any real nightlife, the hunters would have to go farther afield.

They talked for another forty minutes about the possibilities and the prices of cattle and how many they would need to sell to get the ranch back on its feet.

"We'll need to sell enough to pay for construction." Caleb clicked his pencil against his cup. "I'll check some estimates for both a lodge and for just some cabins. We can start small and add on."

"I hate to see you sell too many of those cows." Grady frowned. "They are some fine stock, and you don't come by them very often."

"I have an idea about that," Pierce said.

"No. Absolutely not." Caleb glared at him. "You're not pulling from your retirement fund."

"Not that." Pierce leaned back. "If we sell some cattle to take care of the ranch debt, I have some put away that should be enough to cover the cost of building some cabins to start out. We can consider it a loan, and the ranch business will pay it back as guiding takes off. If it's as lucrative as you suggest, that can happen in a few years and I'm not using that money right now, anyway."

By the time they'd come to an agreement, had breakfast with their mom and seen Kianna off to school, Pierce was itching to get over to Pete's. Silvia hadn't left him. She hadn't. He kept that mantra going throughout his drive to their house.

No one was home. Even Jeanne didn't answer the door. He stood on the porch looking out toward the mountains, where he and Silvia had so much fun hiking. Where they'd taken

Kianna to the fire tower. Where he wanted to take a million more trips with his girls.

Because they belonged together.

He climbed into the truck and headed for town. They had to be at the Chuckwagon. Maybe both Pete and Jeanne were well enough to be there. Silvia must have arrived home in time to pick them up for opening.

The parking lot was pretty full when he pulled in. He recognized most of the vehicles. Several belonged to the regulars, those retirees who liked to meet up at the restaurant and talk about whatever struck their fancy.

The clatter of pans greeted him as he stepped inside. The aromas of bacon and pancakes, sweetness and grease, had him wishing he'd waited to eat.

Pete waved to him from behind the counter, where he'd just put a plate down for a customer.

"Hey, Pete. They've got you working." Pierce patted the older man on the shoulder.

"Just for the morning. What can I get you?" The older man had a sparkle in his eyes Pierce hadn't seen in a while.

"I'm looking for Silvia. Is she in the kitchen or the office?"

Pete's face fell. "Neither. She left yesterday. She's meeting her agent in Phoenix so they can get her book back on track. Jeanne and I told her we'd fill in here. I don't know when she'll be back."

The wheels of her suitcase clattered on the rough pavement of the parking lot. Silvia clicked the key fob and the tailgate of the SUV began its slow rise as she approached. She slung her bags inside and then climbed into the driver's seat, rested her head back and closed her eyes.

She had slept little last night in the motel. Some school team had stayed on the same floor, and those kids did not know when to quit. They'd called up and down the hallway into the wee hours of the morning, despite their chaperone's attempts at corralling them. She'd have slept in, but Marissa expected her at their nine o'clock meeting.

Coffee. She needed coffee. At least Marissa had chosen an upscale coffee shop for their talk. Maybe they'd have a scone or something, and her brain would wake up. She didn't know if she'd be able to discuss the book or the future of her writing. *God, please guide me in this.*

A niggle of guilt wormed deep inside her. She hadn't told Jeanne or her father much about what she was doing, just that she was meeting her agent. She'd prayed. Felt the nudge of God to go to this meeting when Marissa called to say she'd be in Phoenix. She'd made arrangements for the day at the restaurant, surprised when everything fell into place, and made a four-hour drive in just over five hours, thanks to roadwork and an accident blocking the highway.

Jeanne was up to working again, or working part-time. She'd been back the last couple of days but hadn't stayed long. The other cooks were good with filling in, and her dad could run everything from the front. He might even enjoy being in charge again. She hoped.

Marissa sat at a corner table in the back of the coffeehouse. Silvia wove through the tables and put her laptop case on the opposite chair.

"Silvia, so good to see you again." Marissa stood to give her a hug. Her short blond bob fit her lean face. Compared to Silvia, who looked like a herd of cows had run her over, Marissa appeared fresh and as lovely as always. Her breezy top, in a bright splash of mixed colors, went well with her slim black skirt.

"Good to see you. What brings you to Phoenix?" Silvia hung her purse on the chair and opened the coffee-shop app she hadn't used in forever. She looked at her history, chose a drink and scone, chose this shop and put in the order.

"My parents decided last month that they were moving to a retirement community in Phoenix." Marissa sank down in her chair and shook her head. "One month. To pack up what they wanted to keep. Put their house on the market. Get rid of everything they didn't want anymore—which was enough to fill a museum."

"Wow. That's a lot. Did they get everything done?" Silvia rose when her name was called.

"Yes. They're here. The house sold. Now, I just have to catch up on work and sleep." Marissa laughed and waved for her to retrieve her order.

By the time she returned, Marissa was on the phone, taking notes on her iPad, her brow slightly furrowed. "I see. Yes, I'll pass that on. I'm meeting with her right now." She nodded a few times and then clicked off the call.

"That was Catherine. I have some good news and some even better news. What would you like first?"

Silvia's mouth went dry. She'd come prepared to fight for what she felt God wanted her to do. To stand her ground and not go back to other countries and adventures, even if that meant the loss of the book sale. If the publisher didn't want her story, she'd look into the option of self-publishing.

"Okay. I guess the good news."

"Catherine loved the idea of using your early dip into extreme sports as a forerunner in the book. It gives the book a different structure and narrative arc that she and the marketing team are excited about. It will show your readers that building up to the type of sports you and Keith did takes time and the willingness to work."

Marissa tapped her pink polished nail against her cup. "However, because Keith is a co-author of some chapters and because Steven is featured quite a bit…she's worried that not addressing what happened will come across poorly. She'd like you to end the book with what happened with Keith and Steven."

"I…" Silvia's body shut down. Her lungs refused to work. Her heart beat a slow bass rhythm.

"Silvia, stop." Marissa's hand on her arm drew her back to the present. "I told Catherine this might be a deal-breaker. Losing your whole family in one accident is difficult to write about. I warned her about that."

"I don't think…" How could she put that agony into words on paper? Words other people would read? Words that would bleed all over the page. Losing her family had been so private. She hadn't even shared the whole story until recently, and then only with Pierce and her dad.

Pierce. Did he know she'd left? Would he understand or jump to conclusions? She should have left a note for him. Or texted to say she'd be back. But she'd been so confused about what to do. Until those teens kept her awake last night and she met with God instead of sleeping.

She sucked in a breath of coffee-scented air. "I don't know that I can do that. I will pray about it and try. Maybe in another year or two, I could work on a different book. More of a memoir about my life with Keith and include the story then."

Marissa's face lit up. "That's exactly what I suggested to Catherine. She is good with you doing that, too. Wonderful."

For the next thirty minutes they talked about the focus of the book, using the white water rapids adventures as the beginning and ending. She'd start with the class I excursion and end with the class V from last year. That had been their last outing before the tragedy that altered her life.

Her agent pulled out a new contract that detailed the

changes they'd made. She went over it with Silvia while they sipped their coffee and split the scone Silvia had purchased.

Her head ached with all the legal speak by the time they finished. How did a person enjoy reading through contracts? And how did they manage to come up with such archaic language instead of just saying outright what they meant? *Thank you, Marissa, for understanding and interpreting.*

"Are you staying over tonight?" Marissa asked as she tucked the papers in her bag. She would submit the few changes, and then the actual signing would happen after those were added.

"I'll probably drive back. It's a long drive, but I left the restaurant in Dad's hands, and I'm not sure that was wise. I don't want him to overdo." Silvia opened her app and thought about ordering another coffee for the drive home but decided to wait.

She folded her arms on the tabletop. "You mentioned something else before we talked about the book. Some other news."

"Oh, yes. The next book. Not the memoir but the next one about your adventures." Marissa clasped her hands together and leaned forward.

"What other book? What adventures? I'm not going around the world anymore." Silvia studied Marissa's twinkling eyes. What was she thinking?

"Catherine is suggesting a book on adventure sports in the western United States. She sees this as a possibility for future books in other parts of the country, but they will all be in the USA. Your blog will help promote the books, and we expect the sales to be excellent."

"But my readers won't follow. Didn't you see the comments on my last post?" She wanted to crawl under the table as she remembered the unkind words. Still, a thread of hope wound through her. She loved adventure sports, but was ready to leave the extreme ones behind.

"I did. But have you read the comments since that first day?" Marissa's smile grew broader.

"No." Silvia opened to her post, scrolled through and gasped.

Chapter Twenty-One

Pierce tugged the reins and stopped his horse on a hill overlooking the herd of Red Angus his father bought from the Cranes. The cows were grazing, their tails swishing at the flies buzzing around. They were healthy and well filled out. Prime for market.

And he had to choose some to sell. A few of the reds and some of the Black Angus, too.

Grady and Caleb pulled their mounts to a stop beside him. Caleb rode the palomino mare he'd wanted, and she gleamed in the early afternoon light.

Grady rode the buckskin he always rode and Pierce had tried a sorrel gelding with a blond mane and tail. A beautiful horse and well-trained.

He looked over at the foreman. "How do we choose, Grady? I don't want to get rid of any of them."

"I hear you." Grady folded his hands on the pommel of his saddle. "You don't want to sell any that are having problems, but I think all these cows are in top form. Your dad kept the best."

"I found a buyer in Kansas who'll take ten head. He might take some blacks, too." Caleb lifted his hand and ran it through his hair before settling the cowboy hat back in place. "Do you think ten will be enough?"

Pierce considered the debt they faced, the money he had

saved and what they needed for the cabins. "Let's cull out six, along with some blacks, and see how that goes. I think it will be enough. We have the sale price from the calves, which was a healthy amount."

"Okay." Grady nodded. "That will leave us forty-four head of the Red Angus left. I suggest next year we keep the heifers from these cows to build the herd."

"Good idea." Pierce nodded, already planning how to build on the higher-quality stock and eventually replace their medium-quality beeves with the best.

They spent the next two hours separating the cows and getting them corralled and ready to load in the truck. Grady and Caleb would come out with some hands to bring them closer to the ranch house, ready for the buyer to pick up.

Meanwhile, Pierce intended to shower and spend the evening working on the dollhouse after Kianna went to bed. And nursing his wounded heart.

He'd considered going after Silvia, but he had no idea where to find her. And if she was back on the road so she could have new adventures to write about, what could he say to that? Plus, he wasn't a single man with no responsibilities anymore. He had his mother and Kianna. Even Caleb. And he'd given his word to his dad. He had the ranch to build again.

By the time he entered the house, Kianna was home from school, chattering about what she'd done and showing him all the stickers and notes that said "good job!" on her papers. She'd finally made friends and seemed to be settling in, a great relief to him.

He sat down to dinner, but his mom's cooking tasted like straw today. Putting on a good front took energy, and there were some things he simply didn't have the energy for.

"Mom, I'll read to Kianna and get her settled in bed. Then I'm going out to the workshop. Message me if you need me."

The look she gave him said she wanted to talk. He just shook his head, and she backed off.

After Kianna was asleep, he headed to the workshop, flipped on the lights and lifted the blanket from the portion of the dollhouse he'd been working on. He'd already divided the rooms and applied the siding. Pete knew how to get the scalloped eaves to look right. They could talk tomorrow. Tonight, he planned to work on the roof.

Instead, he sat in the chair, head in his hands, trying to pray. Trying to find some meaning in life. Trying to figure out why Silvia had left without a word to him.

With no indication she cared about him.

The door to the shop opened. He gritted his teeth. Tonight he needed to be alone, not holding a conversation with his brother as they worked together. This pity party was for him alone.

The footsteps stopped. He almost laughed. God didn't want him to have a pity party. He had a plan, and Pierce had to trust that it was a good one.

He cleared his throat. "What are you working on tonight, Caleb?"

"If you think I'm Caleb, you might need your eyes checked."

He swung around and almost fell off his stool. "Silvia. I thought…"

"I know. I left again. Without letting you know." She pulled her jacket tight in front. "It was only one night. I hoped you wouldn't even realize I was gone."

"Your dad said you had a meeting with your agent. That you were getting back to your writing. Which means…"

She shifted. Shoved her hands in her pockets. Licked her

lips. "I had a meeting in Phoenix, true. Listen, I have something to say. Will you hear me out?"

He stood and faced her.

"All my life, I wanted to travel. To see the world. Experience things you don't find here in this small town with people who care about you but also know all your business." She shook her head. "I loved doing extreme sports with Keith. Meeting new people. Seeing different countries and cultures. Connecting with like people from all over the world. Writing about it in my blog." She took a hesitant step toward him.

Pierce stood frozen, waiting for the bad news.

"When I came back here to help Dad, my only thought was that I needed to get back out there. My goal was to leave and continue the extreme adventures in Keith and Steven's memory. But I've come to a realization."

"What realization?" His hoarse rasp echoed in the workshop.

"I realized that was Keith's goal. His dream. Mine was always about traveling and meeting people, but mostly it was about family. I loved my family, and that's what I need most.

"I still want to do things like hiking or river rafting. Maybe even some extreme things. But I want to do it from here. With my family." She took another step toward him, her eyes filled with tears and open enough for Pierce to see to her heart.

She stretched out her hand. "I want to do them with you, Pierce. With you and Kianna."

The air in the workshop shimmered with emotion. Silvia held her breath. She'd hurt him. Again. Wasn't that what she always did? Would he forgive her this time? Would he believe her?

Would he be able to trust that she was telling the truth? Was baring her heart for the first time in years enough?

He took her outstretched hand but didn't pull her close. Just wrapped her fingers in his large hands and held on. His throat worked hard as he swallowed. His chest gave a hitch.

"Silvia." Her name on his lips, said in that way, made her feel cherished. He closed the distance between them, and wrapped his arms around her as if he'd never let her go. Maybe he wouldn't. She'd be content with that.

A lifetime with him. The man she'd always loved.

He cupped her cheek. Tilted her head. And then he kissed her. The sweetest touch of lips she'd ever known. A kiss that carried his heart and a promise of all he felt for her.

"Silvia. Baby." He kissed her again. Wrapped her tight to his chest and buried his face in her hair. "I love you so much. I've never stopped loving you. I'd love to do what you need for your book, but I have to be here for my family, too."

"I know." She drew back. Cradled his strong jaw in her palms. Breathed in the scent of horses and pine and him. "I want to be here, too. To take over the restaurant like Dad wants. I'm done with full-time traveling." And she told him about the book detailing adventures in the western USA.

"We could manage that." He turned his head and kissed her palm. "Let's sit down soon and plan it out. Meanwhile, we have some changes here you should know about."

He led her to the stools where he and Caleb sat when working and settled her on one. "First, I want to ask you something. If you don't mind."

Her heart did a slow waltz at the look in his eyes. She nodded, unable to speak.

He dipped his hand in his pocket and dropped to one knee. She gasped. He flipped open a small box, and she recognized the ring. His mother's engagement ring. The family heirloom.

His mouth was warm as he kissed her left hand, bringing her back to the moment. "Silvia, I have loved you for years.

Even when we were apart, you were there with me. Since coming back to Ashville, I've realized how perfect you are for me. I love your heart for family and friends, your sense of duty, and your work ethic, and your joy of life. You are my heart. Will you marry me?"

A tear dropped to their joined hands. She pressed her lips together to keep from sobbing and nodded. "Yes, Pierce Forester. Yes, I'll marry you."

He stood and pulled her from the stool and twirled her around. Kissed her until she was lightheaded.

They scooted the stools close together, and he told her about the changes they were making to the ranch. The problems they'd had. The hope he had of the twins coming home for a visit and for them to get invested in the ranch.

She told him about her book contract. About her shock when Marissa showed her a whole new set of commenters on her blog who loved the walk in the mountains she'd shared. They wanted more posts about things to do in the USA, since many of them couldn't afford to travel overseas.

They'd just finished a discussion about wedding plans and telling their families when she glanced at the time on her phone. "Pierce, it's after midnight. I have to be at the restaurant early with Dad and Jeanne."

They stood, and he tugged her close for another kiss and hug. "Tell you what. Tomorrow is Saturday. How about I bring everyone for breakfast, and we can tell our families together?"

"Perfect." She dragged on her coat as he grabbed his. At her car, she gave him a last kiss and hug. "See you in the morning."

When she got up after way too little sleep, Silvia dressed quickly and slipped the ring around backward, hoping her dad and Jeanne wouldn't notice. They didn't, and at the restaurant she put on gloves while she worked.

"Is something wrong?" Jeanne gave her a curious stare after Silvia nearly dropped a tray of cookies. For the second time. "I don't know when I've seen you this clumsy."

"I had a little trouble sleeping last night. A lot on my mind." Which was true. Of course, it was that handsome man who'd asked her to marry him that had been on her mind.

She felt the change when Pierce and his family walked into the Chuckwagon. She took the last batch of cookies from the oven to cool and slipped off her gloves. Tingles washed through her, and she couldn't wait to share their news.

Her dad was manning the counter, pouring coffee and chatting with his friends when she came out of the kitchen. Pierce and his family were just sitting down at a back booth. He looked up and grinned at her. Said something to his mom and brother and strode to her.

"Good morning." He leaned down and kissed her cheek. Her dad had already gone over to greet Pierce's mom, so they walked over hand in hand. Pierce cleared his throat, and they all looked over at him.

He smiled down at Silvia for a moment before turning to their family. "Last night I asked Silvia to marry me, and she said yes."

Kianna clapped and jumped up and down. "Miss Silvy will live with us forever and ever now." Everyone laughed and congratulated them as Pierce lifted Kianna to join him and Silvia.

Pierce cradled Silvia against his side—a place that felt so right. A place she intended to stay for as long as God gave them. This rancher had stolen her heart, and the promise of a life with him and his sweet daughter was the best adventure ever.

Epilogue

Six months later

"Mommy, I'm ready." Kianna skidded around the corner into the kitchen, the rhinestones on her pink boots glittering in a ray of sunlight. "Is Daddy here?"

Silvia grinned at her new daughter using mommy and daddy to refer to Silvia and Pierce. She'd started that right after their wedding, making them feel like a family.

Kianna had put on jeans and a T-shirt for their ride today but hadn't brushed her hair. It was still in tousled braids from the night before. "He's getting the horses ready now. Why don't you let me fix your hair. I'm not sure your hat will fit."

Kianna chattered as Silvia brushed her hair out and rebraided the strands. Being married and having a family was better than she remembered. She and Pierce had their wedding on February 14, Valentine's Day, and the day Arizona became a state in the US. From now on, it would be a three-fold holiday for them.

They'd moved in with his mom since her dad was doing fine on his own. She still saw her dad almost every day when she picked him up for work at the Chuckwagon. He and Jeanne had become quite close and he'd built up to working full days three or four times a week.

The kitchen door swung open and Pierce walked in just as

Silvia finished Kianna's braids. "How are my girls?" He lifted Kianna up in the air, making her squeal before he hugged Silvia close and kissed her. "Ready to try your new pony?" He grinned down at his daughter.

"I'm all dressed except for my hat." Kianna patted her head before pointing at the hat rack by the door and her pink cowboy hat that matched her boots for color and bling.

"Everyone will see you coming." Pierce handed the hat to Kianna as he grinned at Silvia. Her stomach swooped at the love in his gaze. Being Mrs. Pierce Forester was the best.

She followed them out the door and down to the barn, where two horses and a pony waited for them. They all mounted up and Kianna led the way across the fields toward the section of the ranch where they were breaking ground today on the new lodge.

"Stay close to us," Pierce called to Kianna and she slowed her pony. He nudged his horse closer to Silvia's and took her hand in his. "I got a call from Ashlyn this morning. Sounds like she and Quinn might come for a visit soon."

"That's wonderful. It was genius sending your mom out for a visit. She's loving her time in California and all the glitz and glitter that goes with Ashlyn and Quinn's show. She did mention she'll be ready to come home soon. Will they come with her?" Silvia glanced at Kianna as she leaned from her pony to pick a tall flower off a weed.

"That's the plan. They won't be in time for the groundbreaking today, but Ashlyn suggested they'll be here this weekend." He squeezed her hand. "Maybe we can talk them into babysitting." He wiggled his eyebrows and she laughed.

They didn't need a babysitter. With Caleb close by, they had plenty of opportunities to have a night out without Kianna, but it might do the twins some good to spend time with their niece.

Thirty minutes later, they topped a rise overlooking the valley where the lodge and cabins would be. The view was breathtaking. A herd of antelope grazed in the grass at the far end of the valley. A stream wended through, near enough to the location of the lodge for trout fishing.

Below them, Grady and Caleb were talking to the crew that were here to prep the land. They rode down and Pierce tied their horses before they made their way over to the others.

"Hey, little princess." Caleb swung Kianna up to straddle his hip. "You're sparkly enough that the fish might jump out of that stream just to get a look."

Kianna giggled before wiggling to get down. She left her hand in Caleb's as he shook hands with Pierce and hugged Silvia. "You sure Mom's okay with us starting without her?"

"She's good with it." Pierce wrapped his arm around Silvia's shoulders. "Let's do this thing."

Silvia took Kianna's hand and stepped back to give the brothers room. They each took a shovel and dug the blades into the dirt. Grady held up his phone and took pictures as they turned over the earth, the start of the new lodge. He'd been asked by the editor of the local newspaper to send pictures to go along with the article Silvia was writing.

The bulldozer fired up to start the real work of preparing the site. They all walked to a safe distance away. Caleb rubbed his jaw. "I sure hope this pans out."

"You did the research." Pierce clapped him on the back.

"You know," Silvia said, frowning as she turned to the three men, "my followers have shown some interest in the mountains around here and doing some of the hikes Pierce and I have gone on. I could advertise the lodge to them."

Pierce's eyes sparkled as he met her gaze. "That's perfect. They could fill in the offseason when there isn't any hunting. That's prime time for hiking."

Caleb and Grady were both excited by the idea and began making plans for that contingency. Pierce slipped his arms around Silvia's waist and pulled her to him. "That, my love, is an excellent idea. I don't know why we didn't think of it before."

Silvia cupped his jaw, tracing her thumb over his chin. "Just you wait and see. Forester Ranch is going to be amazing and productive."

Kianna squealed as the bulldozer blade bit into the soil, peeling it up. Pierce leaned close to Silvia and kissed the side of her head, and she snuggled against him as they watched their future unfold.

* * * * *

Dear Reader,

My family and I often camped in the White Mountains of Arizona. We drove all the back roads and visited the ranger lookouts, saw eagles, bears, deer, elk, bighorn sheep and other wildlife. This area is special to me because of the memories.

I wanted to give you a taste of the countryside and the grandeur of the mountains through Silvia and Pierce's story. Their hurtful background was offset by the peaceful setting and the amazing memories they shared growing up.

My love of the area is reflected in their story. Their return to love as they overcome the damage to their hearts is something many of us face. I hope Silvia and Pierce's story touches your heart as it did mine.

Nancy J. Farrier

Get up to 4 Free Books!

**We'll send you 2 free books from each series you try
PLUS a free Mystery Gift.**

FREE
Value Over
$25

Both the **Love Inspired®** and **Love Inspired® Suspense** series feature compelling
novels filled with inspirational romance, faith, forgiveness and hope.